Pageants of Despair

The Nautilus Series

Pageants of Despair

DENNIS HAMLEY

Paul Dry Books

Philadelphia 2006

First Paul Dry Books Edition, 2006

Paul Dry Books, Inc.
Philadelphia, Pennsylvania
www.pauldrybooks.com

Text type: Berthold Walbaum Book
Display type: Quadraat Sans Bold
Composed by P. M. Gordon Associates
Designed by studio ormus

1 3 5 7 9 8 6 4 2
Printed in the United States of America

Library of Congress Cataloging-in-Publication Data
Hamley, Dennis.
   Pageants of despair / Dennis Hamley. – 1st Paul Dry Books ed.
      p. cm. – (Nautilus series ; 2)
   Summary: Traveling north from London to stay with relatives after
his mother's accident, twelve-year-old Peter meets a strange man with
whom he journeys back five hundred years to a performance of religious
plays in which the youth's role determines the fate of those around him.
   ISBN-13: 978-1-58988-028-3 (alk. paper)
   ISBN-10: 1-58988-028-5 (alk. paper)
   [1. Mysteries and miracle plays – Fiction. 2. Time travel – Fiction.
3. England–Fiction.] I. Title. II. Series: Nautilus series (Paul Dry
Books) ; 2.
   PZ7.H18294Pa 2006
   [Fic] – dc22

                                        2006001447

ISBN-13: 978-1-58988-028-3
ISBN-10: 1-58988-028-5

For Peter and Mary

My grateful thanks are due to Form I Red
of the Leon Comprehensive School, Bletchley,
Milton Keynes, who accepted my intrusion
into their midst, listened patiently to the early stages
of this story, and helped me find a title for it.

CONTENTS

Pageants
of Despair

— 1 —

A DEPARTURE AND A MEETING

In the cold December rain, the big blue diesel eased its load of coaches out of King's Cross Station.

Peter stood at the door of the first coach, his head through the open window. The right side of his face became numb with the stinging rain as he watched the gravely waving figure of his father on the platform recede.

As the train entered the Gasworks Tunnel, Peter pushed the window up and went to his seat in the otherwise empty coach. His sandwiches, *The Railway Magazine,* and *Football Monthly* were on the table; his case, a blue quilted anorak stuffed roughly inside, was on the rack above, where his father had stowed it only a little while before.

He sat down and stared sightlessly at his magazines. Slowly, life came back into his face. The train, its huge diesel engine throbbing very close, picked its way cautiously toward Finsbury Park: Peter felt a sudden stab of guilty shame at realizing he was enjoying its progress.

And why shouldn't I? he thought.

There came into his mind the picture of a hospital bed, its occupant swathed in bandages; a blood transfusion being given; doctors and nurses looking tense, worried.

But you don't *know* that's what it's like, he said to himself. That's only what you've seen on television. But they wouldn't let you go to the hospital. So you don't *know* that's what it's like.

He opened *The Railway Magazine*. But the thoughts which came into his mind would not let him concentrate.

You may as well enjoy the journey. You can't do anything to help at home; that's why they've shoved you on the train to Dunfield all on your own – you're best out of the way. Anyway, you've never had a proper train journey before, so make the most of it while you can.

He doggedly turned over the pages – but to no purpose. Whether he liked it or not, his mind was going to try and piece together the previous sixteen hours – since the time he had been watching television the night before and his father had said to him, "Your mother will be home soon. Why don't you save her a bit of work and get yourself to bed, ready for when she comes in?"

Three days before Christmas is not the time for arguing, thought Peter – though it was an argument he and his father often had on the nights his mother was out at her exercise class.

"Come on, Peter. She'll be soon home – she's only got to cross the park from the Church Hall."

So Peter had washed, cleaned his teeth, and scuttled off up to his bedroom, feeling quite self-righteous.

But his mother did not come home.

And from then on, everything had become confused. For the rest of the night was a cacophony of police-car sirens, people in and out of the house, urgent voices. Soon, Peter could stand it no more – whatever was happening, he seemed to have been forgotten.

He went downstairs – and heard, from the kitchen, an only half-familiar voice say, "Well, I think he's too young to be told all of it."

He opened the door.

"Where are Mum and Dad?" he said.

Three people were there; the couple from next door and the woman from over the road.

"Your Dad's all right, Peter. He's at the hospital," said the woman from next door.

"That was a damn stupid thing to say," said her husband.

Peter said nothing.

"You see, Peter," said the husband. "Your mother's had – well, she's had an accident."

"But she'll be all right," said the woman from over the road brightly. "They're very clever these days. She'll be all right, you mark my words."

Peter still said nothing. There was nothing he wanted to ask of these people. So he went back to his bedroom and put the light on. He sat down on the side of his bed and looked at all the objects which until an hour before had been parts of a well-ordered existence, thoroughly understood: his desk, his football portraits, his books, his plastic models – especially "Evening Star," the half-finished railway engine, with its brunswick green boiler and silver connecting-rods, already looking massively impressive.

How long he sat there he did not know. It was very late when a car drew up outside. Peter could hear his father's voice as the neighbors went out, so he rushed downstairs. He saw his father and a policeman enter; the policeman was holding his father's arm, as if he could not stand on his own. Peter was shocked at his father's drained, grey face and red-rimmed eyes.

"I've brought him home," said the policeman. "He can't do any more at the hospital."

"What's happened?" said Peter.

"Has nobody told you?" said the policeman.

Peter's father sat down on a kitchen chair, his head in his hands. The policeman looked embarrassed, as if given a job he had not bargained for. He cleared his throat.

"Well," he said. "It's your mother. When she was crossing the park. There were some yobboes around. They set on her and they – well, they beat her up."

Peter stared at him.

"We call it mugging," said the policeman, as if he thought more explanation was needed. "They ran off with her handbag. Someone disturbed them or it might have been worse."

Peter looked at his father, who had not moved.

The policeman continued, obviously hating every minute of it. "She's unconscious and she lost a lot of blood."

"Will she be all right?" asked Peter.

"Nobody knows. Not for a long time yet." The policeman's tone changed; it became more business-like. "Best go back to bed. Try to get some sleep. The hospital will let us know."

After that, it had all been like a dream. A night of disturbed snatches of sleep; a morning spent with a schoolfriend down the road who made heroic but vain efforts to cheer him up and keep his mind off things; then, at midday, his father coming in and speaking at last.

"I've fixed it up. Tom and Elsie up in Dunfield will have you for a while. Get ready; there's a train in two hours' time."

"But I want to stay here. I want to see Mum."

"You're going to Dunfield. It's all fixed."

Dunfield. Where Mum came from – where she and Dad had met, in fact. Peter had never been up there to Yorkshire – but he knew Uncle Tom and Auntie Elsie well enough, for they had often come down south to visit.

"What about Christmas?"

"You'll have it up there. You'll get two Christmasses in the end."

They packed a case together; Peter chose some books, decided not to take "Evening Star," feeling somehow that it was good to have unfinished work to come back to – and then changed his clothes. He made a point of wearing his new black shoes with the leopard tracks moulded into the sole. He remembered his mother talking when he bought them. "You're twelve – you're too old for that sort of thing now." But he had insisted, and the memory of his insistence made him recall why he was leaving. His newfound excitement evaporated.

A quick meal and a packet of sandwiches for later, then a scaring drive through London to King's Cross, his father's fingers showing white on the steering-wheel, betraying nervousness and worry.

"She'll be all right, Peter. She'll be all right," he kept saying, until Peter was sure he didn't believe it.

When they were on the station and walking along the line of blue and grey coaches, his father said, "Tom and Elsie will meet you at the other end. And I'll ring up when there's something to tell. And don't worry. Mum wouldn't want you to."

So here he was, sitting alone in the front coach of the Leeds train, calling at Peterborough, Grantham, Newark, Retford, Doncaster, Dunfield, and Leeds, gathering speed through the northern suburbs behind its Brush Type 4, Class 47 diesel, and taking him further away from the awful fact which lay like a lump at the back of his mind and which nothing could alter.

"'Tis a terrible thing not to know," said a voice.

"Yes," said Peter unthinkingly.

Then he looked up to see a man in the seat opposite; a man with a leathery face and dark, deep eyes. How did he get there? thought Peter. He felt a shiver of alarm.

"There's much to happen yet," said the man. His voice was deep, guttural, strange.

He must have come from the rear coaches and sat down while I was thinking, Peter decided.

The train went quickly through Potter's Bar: the station buildings passed by as little oblong shapes each seen for a split-second. The neighing of the engine's two-tone horn sounded very close.

"Those are t'first two notes of 'On Ilkley Moor baht 'at,'" said the man.

"Yes," said Peter.

"The driver must be a West Riding man. He's probably glad he's going home," said the man. The voice now seemed strongly north-country.

"He's either King's Cross or Doncaster," said Peter, hoping he didn't sound too knowledgeable.

"I would think a London man would sound t'horn t'other way round," said the man.

"You mean like the beginning of 'Colonel Bogey'?" said Peter.

"This man's going home," was the reply.

The connecting door at the end of the coach suddenly slid open and the ticket-collector appeared. Peter held out the half return to Dunfield and it was clipped.

"Are you on your own?" said the ticket-collector.

"Yes," said Peter, presuming the remark asked him how he was travelling.

"First stop after Doncaster," said the ticket-collector. "I'll see you get off all right."

He walked up the coach, saw nobody else was there and went back the way he had come, totally ignoring the large man in the corner.

"Haven't you got a ticket?" said Peter.

"I have no need of one," said the man.

Obviously, thought Peter, he works for the railway and is so well known that the ticket-collectors don't bother to ask him any more.

"You must be very important," Peter said.

"I suppose I may have been once," said the man.

Yes, he looks old enough to be retired, thought Peter.

"What art tha reading, lad?" asked the man.

Peter held up *The Railway Magazine*. "I expect you know much more about it than I do," he said.

"Why should I?" said the man.

"Well, you used to work for the railway," said Peter.

"What made you think that?"

"Because you haven't . . ." started Peter, and then stopped.

"I think I would have liked to," said the man.

Peter wondered if he was like one of the nineteenth-century dukes who had free railway passes and private stations in return for letting the track go across their land. But surely British Rail had got rid of all that sort of thing. He turned back to his magazine and was on the point of becoming lost in a vanished world of steam engines.

"Why be so fond of the past?" said the man.

Peter's concentration broke.

"They're not all gone," he said. Obviously the man could see the photographs in the magazine. "I've seen a few engines preserved and still running."

"But 'tis not the same as seeing them all the time."

"I might not appreciate them so much," said Peter.

"But if tomorrow all t'steam engines were back, wouldst thou not be pleased?"

"Yes. But that's daft. It won't happen, however much I'd like it to. Time can't go back. We couldn't start again."

If only we could, he thought. I'd like to start again just from last night. Things might turn out differently.

"Think about it," said the man.

Yes. If only last night could come again and they could stop mother going to the exercise class, or his father would pick her up in the car. It was like a story read for a second time in the hope that the ending might be changed. Or a film seen twice – couldn't the second time the gunfight at the end be avoided? Or – and the sight appeared clearly to him – every time he saw an action replay of that last-minute goal that had beaten his favorite team and left him desolated.

"Yes," said the man, as if reading Peter's thoughts. "This time it might be different."

"But it can't be," cried Peter, suddenly feeling alarmed.

"But what if it is?" insisted the man.

Peter was silent.

The train bustled through Sandy. Peter peered through the window looking for the bridge which carried the old Oxford-to-Cambridge branch over the main line.

"Well?" said the man.

"That's stupid," said Peter.

"Is it?"

Peter took out his packet of sandwiches and ate them, offering none to the man. He tried to read *The Railway Magazine.*

But he couldn't. He was worried. Had the man really known he had seen again in his mind's eye the television picture of a goalkeeper trying to stop a certain goal? And why was he himself so worried about something so stupid? But was it stupid? What *would* happen if just once, the repetition of something were different from the original. It was a mind-boggling idea: Peter's mind somehow could not get hold of it.

"And what about plays?" the man continued, a note of excitement coming into his voice. "What about plays?"

Peter's eyes strayed to the communication cord. But £25 seemed a fortune, so he decided to stick it out.

10

The man's voice grew more and more urgent, as if he was saying something he had to get out of his system at all costs.

"What about plays? I know tha went to pantomimes when tha wert smaller. What about the Demon King? I'll wager tha shouted 'Look out' to t' Dame when t' Demon King crept up on her. It were like real, weren't it? But he weren't a Demon King – he were a man; a man like thi father, or – or like me."

Peter thought that if the Demon King was like him, there wasn't much difference between pantomime and real life. He was, the truth to tell, becoming frightened.

But it was an interesting point the man had brought up. It deserved an answer.

"Of course I thought it was real," he said. "But I was only six then. I'm twelve now. I know it's only make-believe. So do grown-ups: they just go to watch."

"Why?" asked the man.

"Why what?" said Peter.

"Why should they go to watch if 'tis only make-believe? What's t' point?"

"I don't know, if you put it like that," said Peter.

They passed Huntingdon: Peter knew they were approaching a stretch of line where it would be worthwhile timing the train with his watch.

The country was flat and dotted with stretches of floodwater after the heavy rain. The absence of rail-joints and the bareness of fenland outside the window made it very difficult to have any real idea of the speed of the train; even so, Peter's excitement mounted as the next four mileposts whisked by with exactly forty seconds between them.

"We're averaging ninety," he said to the man. "If we'd got a Deltic instead of a Brush we'd be doing the ton easily."

"What about the villain in a play?" said the man.

Peter tried not to listen.

"What about t' villain? The actor who takes the part is an ordinary man – but he has to look like a villain and sound like one. Or nobody will listen to him. And if he looks like one and sounds like one, then he may feel like one. What if he *likes* feeling like one? What if he takes t' blanks out of his gun and puts live bullets in it? What if he shoots t' hero with them? What if the villain says, 'Every night I go on t' stage and every night I'm beaten. This night I'll win.' Then 'tis not a play. 'Tis real life. What of *Macbeth*? What if one night Macbeth won?"

This speech came out very quickly, and by the time it had finished, Peter had forgotten all about his watch and the speed of the train. He stared at the man in amazement.

"Who are you?" he said.

The man didn't answer for a moment. Then he said, "I hope I've not frightened thee."

"No," said Peter faintly. But his heart was thumping strangely.

There was no doubt – for a moment he had been frightened. Something in the man's peculiar, deep voice had riveted him – a strange urgency. But the fright passed. Peter felt that if he could have a proper conversation he would end up by liking him very much.

He looked again at the man. Yes, his eyes were dark, deep, and gentle. He was balding considerably. Afterwards, Peter could never remember what the man was wearing – but it seemed like some sort of long cloak, not unlike the cassock worn by the Vicar at home, but, instead of black, a darkish brown, and made of very much rougher material.

"Yes," said the man. "I were important once. I were important in Dunfield. That's where thou'rt going, isn't it?"

"What did you do in Dunfield?" asked Peter.

"I wrote part of a cycle."

"You don't write cycles: you ride them," said Peter.

"What dost tha think a cycle is?" asked the man.

"It's a bike, of course," said Peter.

"No. A cycle is a series of plays. I thought that was what tha called them now. And I wrote some of them. I see I shall have to start again."

Peter wondered if in fact he was very stupid.

The next question the man asked nearly rocked him out of his seat.

"Dost tha believe people can come back out of the past?"

"I don't know," was all Peter could say. "How do you mean?"

"Dost tha believe that a man can really be living at one time but can go into another century if he wants to – or if he has to?"

Peter thought he had better try to treat the question sensibly.

"They do it in space-fiction – in time machines and things," he said.

"Ah," said the man, smiling. "Now it is thee that is puzzling me."

"You must be living at some other time if you've never heard of that," said Peter.

"Yes," said the man.

Peter's mind was in a whirl. The man obviously meant it.

"You mean . . . " he started. That would explain a lot – the reason for having no ticket; the reason for not being seen by the ticket-collector; the reason for appearing so strangely in the corner seat at all. Yet the man had heard of "On Ilkley Moor baht 'at" and knew about pantomimes, guns, and bullets.

The metallic, grinding roar of the train's brakes being applied sounded through the coach. They were coming into Peterborough.

"Say no more for a while," said the man.

Peter was dazed. The train stopped with a squeal of brakes. The dull clatter of the diesel engine ticking over, the sound of footsteps and voices of people on the platform, the muffled indecipherable boom of the station announcer's voice – all the things he would normally have taken such delight in – might as well not have existed for Peter as his mind tried to grapple with this new and shocking idea. He was sitting opposite and had been talking with a man who did not live in his world; who was not real; who could not be a human being: who must be dead; who thus must be – and this hammered through Peter's head – *must be,* MUST BE a ghost.

"Nay, I'm no ghost," murmured the man – and once again Peter wondered if he were somehow answering his thoughts. "I am still living my own life of many years ago, and before this day is out I will be back in my rightful time."

Although the platform was crowded and although many people boarded the train, nobody tried to enter the front coach. Even when the train had started again and was clacking busily over the pointwork at the north end of Peterborough Station, Peter and the man were still alone.

"And now I shall tell thee why," said the man.

Peter felt a curious thrill in his stomach. It was the feeling he had when his father took him to Stamford Bridge to watch Chelsea – when the buzz of the crowd stopped; little hazes of tobacco smoke would drift across the bare pitch in the autumn air; everybody would crane forward and a tension would pass through them all as the two teams ran out of the players' tunnel, crossed the greyhound track, and walked on to the grass for and afternoon of glorious uncertainty.

– 2 –

GILBERT

"I didn't want to come here," said the man. "I had to."

He stared out of the window for a minute, drumming his fingers on the table, and then said, "Thou art going to Dunfield. So am I. So is t' engine-driver. And we cannot be there quickly enough. But I shall be there long before all of thee. I'd not have come here anyway. I had to."

The train was accelerating toward Little Bytham and one of the greet high-speed stretches of railway line. In spite of his shock, Peter began to look out for the place where *Mallard* broke the world speed record. Then something occurred to him which made him wonder whether he was after all being tricked.

"If you're supposed to have lived so long ago," he said, "how come you know some things and not others? You knew about guns and things but you say you don't know what science fiction is. I think you're having me on."

"I swear I'm not," replied the man. "I have been here a long time. I came to find the answer to a question. This age should have known, so far ahead is it of mine. But I was wrong. Five hundred years have gone by. But it all seems cloudier, not clearer. Soon I go back. Already I feel the gap in time is waiting for me."

"What is your name?" asked Peter.

"Why should I tell thee? Tha canst call me by the Christian name some people in thy age think I had. Call me Gilbert."

"Is that your name?"

"Tha might find out for thyself later on," smiled Gilbert.

"You still haven't told me what you're going back to and how you got here – or why you came at all."

"No," said Gilbert. "It would be very strange and uncomfortable to thee, I suppose, the life I am really used to and to which I look forward again so much."

And then Gilbert leaned forward in his seat, put his elbows on the table, and clasped his hands together under his chin as he told Peter his story.

Gilbert said that he lived in Dunfield five hundred years before – "But a Dunfield much different from the one thou art going to," he added.

It would be a tiny town to Peter – but very big for the time. There were no coal mines nearby, no mills and factories. There were people quietly following their trades, growing their crops, and tending their sheep. The sheep were the most important things – they gave meat and they gave wool, the staples of life.

"My people," said Gilbert, "live hard. I don't think tha could stand it. But there are many in this world nowadays, in other lands, who live worse."

Then he told Peter of the series of plays that were performed in Dunfield every year: of how all the trades people came together in their Gilds – "like your Unions," said Gilbert – and how each Gild every Whitsun acted a play. He told Peter how there were forty or so of these plays and how, when they were all performed together in order, they told

16

the whole of the Bible story from the Creation to the Day of Judgement.

"Every year?" asked Peter. "Don't they know it yet?"

"'Tis the only chance they get," said Gilbert. "There's little chance of seeing an English bible – and few enough could read it."

He went on to say how the days of the acting of the plays were the great occasions of the year – like a carnival. Everybody came together: some to act, some to watch, some to do both.

"We feel like a real town," said Gilbert. "We feel we belong. We're all doing something worthwhile together; it stops us arguing and fighting among ourselves."

"Do *you* act in them?" asked Peter.

"No. I told thee; I wrote part of a cycle. I started to copy out all the plays because I am a scribe. But I thought a few were little use – so I wrote some new ones. People tell me they are the best. I agree with them. They are."

"Is this why you asked me all those funny questions before?" asked Peter. "About what would happen if the man playing the villain thought he was a villain and made the play different?"

"I'm coming to that," said Gilbert. "I told thee that my people were different. Compared with thee they are like children; they are not stupid – but they know far less. See now, thunder and lightning would never frighten thee; tha'd just read a book to tell thee what it's all about. My people are frightened because they do not know. So they have to explain it to themselves – they say it's God being angry with them – the only thing they can think of which fits the facts. They believe God is everywhere; all round them; controlling everything they do. But, even if God *is* there, life is still nasty. A battle is going on. Good is fighting evil. Light is fighting darkness."

Gilbert looked out of the carriage window. The train was passing a derelict factory, grey and half-ruined.

"I see 'tis still going on," he said.

Peter said nothing. He was thinking about his mother.

"So my plays are important," said Gilbert. "Every year the folk come to act and watch. Every year the plays say, 'look, 'tis all right. This is what happened. Now it happens again. Watch, listen, think on – and maybe thou canst keep going until next year.' But what if one year it never happened?"

"You mean if it rained and you had to cancel them," said Peter.

"No," said Gilbert.

He was silent for a moment. His face looked troubled.

"What if one year Cain really did kill Abel? What if no angel appeared and Abraham *had* to sacrifice Isaac? God would have gone away. What if one year Christ did not rise from the dead? What if one year the good were damned at the Day of Judgement?"

"But they're only plays," said Peter.

"You shouted at the pantomime. You thought it was really happening."

"Part of me did," Peter admitted.

"And so do my folk," said Gilbert.

"But you wrote the plays. If they learn your words and say them right, none of this can happen."

Gilbert sat back in his seat and traced his finger along the aluminum window frame. His face grew thoughtful – as if he was collecting together the facts in his mind before he told his story.

"I wrote them," said Gilbert. "And then I gave them to the actors. I wrote about Cain and Abel, Noah, the Shepherds, Herod, the torturing of Jesus, and the Day of Judgement. I gave each play to the Gild that wanted it. And then the dreams started."

"What dreams?" asked Peter.

The train was slowing for the Grantham stop. Peter saw that Gilbert would say no more until they were on their way again.

It seemed an age before the Brush Type 4 lumbered out of the station. The atmosphere was much quieter here than at Peterborough. A blue diesel multiple-unit squealed into the bay platform opposite their coach; it seemed many miles away. A cold wind blew round the bare lamp-standards and filtered through the slightly open carriage windows. With it entered scraps of sound from the station announcer's voice. The winter darkness on this the shortest day of the year was beginning to close in. Time seemed to drag on its way slowly.

Then the whistle blew and the train drew awkwardly out. Gilbert resumed his story.

"In my play of the Day of Judgement I had invented a character called Tuttivillus. He was a devil – but a funny devil, I suppose. He carried a large horn which he blew to signify the last day of the world. One night I dreamt about him. I worried little about that. But next night I dreamt about him again. And this time he blew his horn. Each night he seemed to be larger and more terrifying: each night he blew his horn louder and louder. One night he had become so huge that all I could see were his glaring, blood-red eyes: all I could feel was breath hot like an open fire."

Peter remembered a painting he had seen of a steam railway engine dropping its fire at night, livid against the blackness; the picture seemed to fit.

"He blew his horn so loud I was totally deafened. Then there was silence. After a minute or so he spoke: a deep,

deep voice that throbbed. I could feel the voice more than hear it."

Peter saw sweat on Gilbert's forehead, as he relived his dream: the realization dawned on him that it was now Gilbert who was afraid.

"What did the devil say?" he asked.

"To start with, words I knew nothing of, in a language I did not understand. All I know is that I hope never to hear the sounds again. Then he spoke in my tongue: 'You have put a weapon in my hands.' Straight away he disappeared – and for some nights I was free.

"I watched the actors rehearse their new plays. At first they were happy. They enjoyed them: they told me how much they got out of them. The rehearsals seemed to be going well. Cain and Abel were a good partnership – brothers in real life as well as in the play. The three shepherds were doing well; Mak the sheep-stealer's performance was coming on nicely.

"Then things began to go wrong. One night I saw Cain and Abel fighting after the rehearsal. I was amazed. These two brothers, apprentice glovers – they'd never argued before. But Cain had blacked Abel's eye and made his nose bleed – and neither of them could explain why. But I knew. 'Twas the play that had split them apart. They were becoming like the real Cain and Abel. Then I found the three who have the shepherds' parts. They are shepherds themselves. In the play I wrote, they find out that Mak has stolen their sheep. We hang a man for that in real life. But not in the play: how could I let three shepherds who have just hanged a man go to the manger to find Christ? So I let them toss Mak up in a blanket. But I found the three of them chasing Mak down the street. If I had not caught them they would have lynched him. They were no more the men I knew. In a curious way they were becoming the characters I had invented

20

– but they were not showing the mercy I had put into their parts. I knew something evil was happening, but what it was I knew not."

Peter remembered that he too wanted to know what was happening. He didn't know what news he would receive when his father rang up; what he would find when he finally returned home. He thought of "Evening Star" still on his desk – then the picture turned into the real "Evening Star" dropping its fire at night and he shivered. He remembered the embarrassed words of the policeman; his father standing lonely on the platform as the train drew out of King's Cross. Already everything that had happened before the train had left King's Cross seemed in another world – in another century. He and the train were the only links; and the train was making him a more and more feeble link with every milepost it passed.

He looked with sympathy at Gilbert. Deep down he felt there was a bond between them that he couldn't quite describe. They were both alone, both lost in a world that had gone wrong round them. They shared the bewilderment of a mystifying journey.

Gilbert's forehead was wrinkled and his right fist, clenched hard and showing white like Peter's father's on the steering wheel, was pressed against it. He spoke.

"I thought and thought. I racked my brains till they ached. Then I started to dream again: but these were different dreams. No devil came to visit me: these dreams seemed from within my own mind. I saw the plays themselves. 'Twas Corpus Christi Day, the day of the procession. I saw the town full of people: life and noise throughout the little streets; a great press of folk from all around coming in for the great holiday. I saw the procession start from the cathedral: priests, actors, people – all happy, chattering, excited, and confident of what was going to happen. I saw them crowd down to the acting area the next day: I saw the stages for each play brought in place round the great circular arena. I saw the people scramble into their places, jostling to get good views. And my heart groaned because I knew what was to happen. The plays started. Lucifer was thrown out of heaven and there was a hush as his curse on God and man sounded out clearly. I saw Cain kill Abel and call to the audience in his exultation. And the audience answered him with cheer on cheer. I saw Abraham and Isaac: no angel came and I saw Isaac lie dead upon the ground. And the shepherds took Mak the sheep-stealer and killed him before the eyes of the people. And they watched, sullen, angry, as the murderers gave their gifts to Christ, their hands still hot with the death of Mak. Still – the crowd watched, with sullen anger. And so the Day of Judgement came, along with the devil with the horn. He blew it – and the crowd suddenly came to life. And shouting, with death in their hearts, they rose up and ran through the mouth of Hell, out of the place, into the town and all around answering the summons. I saw fires started, I heard the crying of those who were trampled under foot and the crying of those they killed. And I heard a shout of 'Our God has gone away.' And I woke with the shout in my ears and there it has remained ever since.

"I rose up troubled and started to walk away from the town toward Doncaster. Fool, I called myself, for writing plays that see into the minds of men. For I was sure that what I had seen would come true."

"Did it?" asked Peter quietly, troubled afresh with thoughts of violence.

"In the time of my world," said Gilbert, "that Corpus Christi Day has not yet come. As I walked I pounded my brains. I tried to see what the future would be like, for I felt there was too great a force against me to stop my dream happening. I wanted to know what difference it would make. If Evil triumphed in Dunfield through my fault, it would spread over the land, over the world, and there would be no man to stop it. And the whole of history would be altered. I thought and thought and thought. I sweated with the power of my thought. And as I walked I felt a blackness come over me: a trance descended and I felt myself taken up on wings. Another power greater than me seemed to take me up and I travelled on in a fog. Somehow I knew what I was to do. Whether I liked it or not someone had chosen me to be the agent to work against the devil with the horn and all he could do. And, just as I expected, I was let down again in the future – but much further forward in time than I had thought to be, and in a world that for a long time was something beyond me to understand.

"For I suddenly found myself sitting down, in a soft seat in front of a table. I was moving and yet sitting still. For a while I was too frightened to lift my eyes. When I did, I looked out of a window beside me – and saw that I had finished my journey to Doncaster. But I was in your world, on a train just like this, going South. This was a year ago. Since then I have moved around thy world, invisible to many but seen by a few – the few like thee, whom I can trust and who would not think me a madman as soon as I open my mouth. I watched, listened, and pondered. I have read every book I can lay my hands on to see a mention of what happened in my dream. But none can I find.

"And this age is so puzzling to me – I cannot tell if 'tis good or evil. I cannot see if all the wars, the death, the violence I see is a result of my dream so that evil has smothered the world, or whether my people were saved and all the comfort, the power, the knowledge – beyond me to comprehend – of your world shows that good is triumphing. I cannot tell, I cannot tell, I cannot tell. So I return to Dunfield, not knowing if the disaster will happen and not knowing how to stop it if it starts."

"Can you get back?" asked Peter.

"Yes," said Gilbert. "At this moment, believe it or not, I am sleeping by the roadside just out of Dunfield. Soon I shall wake up and get to my feet. 'Twill be five hundred years ago and I shall have had a doze of about an hour."

Peter was silent. He wrestled with swirling thoughts that would not find words. Gilbert's vision of disaster and his own of a hospital bed seemed very similar.

At last he spoke in a trembling voice.

"If I went to sleep in this carriage, would I wake up in an hour?"

Gilbert looked at him.

"I did not dare to hope tha'd ask that," he said.

"I don't know why I did," replied Peter. "It's just that I've got a strange feeling that if things work out for you, they'll work out for me. And if I don't come with you, how will I know?"

"If thou shouldst come with me and I am strong enough then thou couldst help me. Nay, lad, I see it now. 'Tis thee I came to fetch. Thou art bound to come with me."

"What can I do?" asked Peter.

"Thou'lt see when we are there. I do not know myself yet. But I feel that whatever happens will be done either by thee or because of thee."

"I will get back here, won't I?"

"I am sure so," said Gilbert. "But I am also sure that how the world seems to thee on thy return will depend on what happens to thee in my world."

Peter thought again: if it works for him it will for me. And he tried to think of what it would be like stepping finally off the train at Dunfield.

He could not envisage it at all: the extraordinary thing was that he did not feel in the least worried by the fact that the end of his journey was to be pushed back indefinitely and that he was now embarking on something which an hour before would have seemed totally ridiculous. Was there a common purpose as well? He quickly thought back over everything that had happened since that morning and felt that it had all been inevitable – that really there was no call for surprise at all. Nothing could have happened differently. There was no question of drawing back.

"Art ready, then, lad?" said Gilbert.

"How do we get there?" asked Peter.

"I do not know; but 'tis time, that I do know – and that we will get our power from any source available to us. Cling hard to my arm."

Arthur Lumb had driven diesels off Doncaster shed on the King's Cross run for seven years. There was hardly a main-line class of locomotive he did not know through and through. He usually drove Deltics but was used enough to the Brush Type 4. Yet he could never account for what happened on that evening just three miles south of Newark.

"It were right strange," he said that night in the pub, a pint of Beverley's Trinity in front of him. "I were just thinking we'd be back nicely for us tea when t' stupid heap of an engine just died on me. We were doin' a good steady sixty-five – no hurry, we were in time – and then she went. Just like that. Engine stopped; lights went out. Useless it were. And we just stood there like fools for an hour till relief came out."

And indeed, for the next hour or so the train did just that – it stood there, useless. Dozens of passengers who could not see to write composed angry letters to British Rail in their heads – others made the best of things and used the quiet and the dark to doze off. The Buffet Car quickly sold out. It was like a shipwreck.

The wind played mournfully round the silent, dark line of coaches in the deepening dusk as the temperature dropped and the sodden landscape began to freeze.

And in the otherwise empty first coach, a little boy, his case by his side and his magazine open on the table in front of him, slept soundly.

– 3 –

AN ENCOUNTER ON THE ROAD

Peter could never really remember what happened to him next. There was a jumble of confused and violent sensations – as if being snatched up in a grasp like a vice and whirled through the air. He felt like a mouse caught up by a hawk; he could see nothing because all around him was a choking grey fog. There was no feeling of time: it could have lasted three minutes or three years for all Peter could remember later. However, there must have been some period of unconsciousness. Peter could never quite place when the fog cleared and he came to his senses. The only way he could describe it was to say, "I was just sitting on the grass."

It was early afternoon. The sun burned down in the still air. The jacket, jersey, shirt, and vest that Peter still had on for a twentieth-century winter felt sweaty and uncomfortable. He took off the jersey and jacket.

Gilbert was sitting on the ground next to him, leaning forward, his hands clasped over his shins and just above his feet. He was deep in thought: his face looked more troubled than ever. He seemed gaunter, darker about the chin –

in fact, thought Peter, he was somehow clearly focused in more detail.

Neither of them spoke. Peter was aware that the silence stretched far beyond them: total emptiness all round on this hot, sultry day. Nearly always, in his life, Peter realized, he had been used to a background rumble – of traffic, of voices, of wireless, aeroplanes, trains. But not now: here was a stillness from which even animal or bird noises seemed excluded – the stillness of the calm before the storm.

It was a disturbing atmosphere: but nothing to the sudden disturbance in Peter's own mind. It felt as though someone punched him in the stomach without warning. He wanted to cry with powerless frustration. Because now he saw what had really happened to him. Horrifying, nightmare thoughts hurled themselves through his mind, thoughts which were impossible to express in words. But gradually there formed the conviction that he had wilfully marooned himself in a world which was not his, at a time which was not his, and all for reasons which, however good they had seemed in the train, now appeared totally ridiculous. He had tagged along with someone who must be a total nut – if he existed at all – and had taken so much notice of him as to let himself be brought into a situation which now seemed totally hopeless.

Peter cast a sideways glance at Gilbert, who was still sitting, quite immobile, staring out into space. As Peter had already noticed he seemed different – darker, rougher, more violent-looking – as if the man he had spoken to in the train had been a different edition of the same person – as if all the rough edges had been smoothed off before but were now reappearing. But Gilbert would be Peter's only link with his real world, and he must put all his trust in him. The thought made him recall his own past – which was five hundred years in the future. He wondered how – and if – he would ever rejoin his own life. Everything that was familiar to him seemed lost: he saw his mother, father, friends, his house, his possessions – all on the other side of a great chasm, totally unbridgeable, never again to be attained. He cried.

Gilbert moved for the first time. He turned his head and looked at Peter, sympathetic but embarrassed. Peter knew there would be no comfort offered which had any meaning – but soon his tears subsided and he felt merely numb.

"Listen," said Gilbert.

In spite of himself, Peter listened. Now his ears did begin to pick out individual sounds. Birdsong seemed to travel for miles, and underneath was a faint baa-ing of sheep, like the drone bass of a pair of bagpipes.

"Most of all I hated thy age for killing all sounds worth listening to," said Gilbert.

Peter's eyes began to take in his surroundings. He saw what looked to him a curiously disorderly landscape. They were sitting beside a rutted track of beaten earth and stone (is this what Gilbert called a road? thought Peter) and all around were low, yet well-wooded hills. There seemed no system in the layout of the trees: it was not forest, nor was it open land. The trees were just dotted here and there. The sight was alien to Peter who had instinctively expected the countryside to be divided neatly up into fields and did not realize that three hundred and more years were to pass before hedges would be laid.

But these were no more than fleeting impressions. More important matters were crossing and recrossing Peter's mind.

"Who brought us here?" he said.

"I do not know."

"Is there some enemy?"

"Yes."

"Who?"

"I know not who. But I know *what*. Yet I can put no name to it."

"It's not all a mistake, is it?" said Peter.

"No. Thou'rt here, and if 'twere not meant, thou'ld still be on t' train reading."

Gilbert's voice had changed as well. It was harsher, deeper, jagged somehow. And though Peter had been aware of a north-country accent in the train, he was aware now of something much stronger – not now like the speech he was used to from Uncle Tom and Auntie Elsie, but broader, more difficult to understand – almost foreign. Some sounds Peter had great difficulty in understanding at all.

"Aye, thou art meant to be here."

This did not comfort Peter.

"What am I supposed to do?" he said.

"Look over to the west, toward the sun," said Gilbert. "What is there?"

"A town on a hill. With a great spire in the middle."

Two miles away to the west was a long, low but commanding hill. The outline of roofs on its skyline could be clearly seen – and in the middle the spire of the great church shot upwards.

"That is Dunfield," said Gilbert. "There now we go."

"But who will you say I am? It'll look a bit odd you carting me about the place in a shirt and trousers if you're only supposed to have been gone for an hour or two."

"I shall say I met a boy from a travelling troupe of actors from the south. He had been badly treated and had run away. I saw him on the road and helped him. He was born in London so nobody will think it odd if they understand nothing he says. But he is a professional, so he has skills we can use in our plays. He will work for us – and will want to stay in Dunfield over Corpus Christi for professional interest."

"Is this me?" asked Peter. "What's that about skills?"

30

"Now I shall go to fetch clothes for thee – to a priory not far off where I am well known. Hide while I am gone and sleep if thou canst. Tha must keep out of sight, for if people see thee as thou art, they will think thee a devil out of hell."

Gilbert walked off down the road with a long swinging stride. Peter lay down behind a clump of bushes. He suddenly felt very tired. It was the first time he had been alone since he was last in his bedroom. He stretched himself out on the grass. It smelt fresh. The sun filtered delicately through the leaves of the bushes. Peter felt comfortable and relaxed, despite the foreboding sultriness in the air.

When he woke up an hour or so later he felt much better. Gilbert was standing over him holding a bundle of dark-brown cloth.

"What is it?" asked Peter. "It looks like gear for a midget monk."

"It is," said Gilbert. "They take them in at seven years old here. Nobody who sees thee in this will look at thee twice."

"Well, what am I, then? A monk or an actor?"

"An actor. But thou wert in such a bad state when I met thee that tha needed some new clothes. 'Tis what I told them at t' priory."

Peter slipped the habit on. It was of rough serge-like material. He tied the rope around him in a clumsy knot. Meanwhile, Gilbert tied the jacket and jersey into a loose bundle and looped it over a stick he had broken off the bush behind which Peter had slept. So on they walked, Peter carrying the stick over his shoulder. They looked like ecclesiastical tramps.

As they plodded on, Gilbert told Peter more of what was to happen. He told how on Corpus Christi Day itself there would be a vast procession, starting very early in the morning. There would be a service in the great church. Then all the Pageants – the separate stages for each play, fitted with wheels and so able to be towed from place to place – would move off round the boundaries of the town, for they were too wide easily to negotiate the narrow streets. At every stopping place, the actors on each Pageant would group themselves into positions – as still tableaux – which would give the gist of the story of the play they were to act in.

"Like the stills outside cinemas," said Peter. "They're giving a sort of trailer."

Gilbert told him how next day the Pageants would be pulled along to the great acting area. And there the real performances would begin.

"And what am I supposed to do?" asked Peter. "Watch them?"

"Thou art an actor. So tha must act. What else?"

"Why?" cried Peter in horror and dismay. "I can't act. I've never done any. Besides, I couldn't learn the lines in a day or two."

"Listen," said Gilbert. "Does tha remember what I said about the rehearsals for my plays?"

"Yes. You said they started fighting each other, as if they thought they were the characters they were acting."

"So?"

"I don't know. It sounded all right in the train, but it seems a load of rubbish now."

"Then think on. What was I afraid of? What did the devil in my dream make me dread as he blew the horn?"

"That the plays would stop being plays and really happen."

"And then what?"

"Well, that all the audience would rush off and break the place up."

"Is that all?"

"I suppose so."

32

"And would that be worth it all? To have me snatched out of my own times into thine? And for thee to be brought back here?"

"Well, I don't know, do I? I don't know anything. Except I wish I wasn't here."

"It matters, Peter," said Gilbert. "It matters."

"Show me, then," said Peter.

"Ah, 'tis so hard to make thee understand what I cannot know myself," said Gilbert. "But try, lad, try to see what I mean."

"Show me," repeated Peter, whose bafflement was turning to anger.

"Say that thou wert back at home and standing in front of t' biggest building in town and tha said to it, 'I don't believe thou art there' and so it fell down in front of thee, a big heap on t' ground."

"That's daft," said Peter.

"But what if it happened?"

"I don't want to listen," said Peter.

"By God, I'll make thee," Gilbert suddenly roared, so loud that Peter jumped. "'Tis what I said before on t' train. Tha've got to listen. If yon building fell down like I said, it would be like nothing you took for granted were there any more. And then what wouldst tha think?"

"That the world had gone crazy. Or I had," said Peter.

"And if the Corpus Christi Plays turn out wrongly, t' world will go crazy for the people here. If the stories they expect to see are denied and twisted by the characters themselves, everything they believe in is finished."

"But lots of people don't believe in God. And they seem all right," said Peter.

"'Tis all right in thy century," said Gilbert. "I told thee, you think you can explain everything to satisfy thyselves. We cannot. It means to us the whole of the life that we know.

I said it before – the cry of 'Our God has gone away' haunts my dreams. And something, someone, somewhere, wants it to happen. And we must stop it."

"But why should I have to act in the plays?" Peter asked.

"Because the best way of stopping it happening is to have one actor who knows the danger and who can be there to make it come out all right on the stage."

Peter was silent. Even if he could act, it seemed a terrible responsibility, especially as he had not the slightest idea of what the plays were like. Once again, he felt a deep feeling of frustration.

"This is all ridiculous," he burst out bitterly. "First of all there's only you saying anything wrong's going to happen. And even if there is, I don't see how me prancing around forgetting lines I don't even understand is going to stop it. It's a total load of rubbish and if I knew how to get back on that train I'd be there now, I tell you."

Gilbert looked grieved. "I thought we were united," he said.

"Now I'm here it seems different," said Peter.

Gilbert trudged on. The spire of Dunfield Church seemed no nearer. Peter stayed behind. He was thinking. Why had he so much wanted to come? It had seemed important in the train. Gilbert's story had been fantastic – but curiously it had convinced him. Why? A blurred vision of a dark figure with fiery, livid eyes and the faint sound of a long, clear, high note like a trumpet entered his mind. He ran after Gilbert.

"If we don't stop it happening, what then?" he asked.

"Like tha said, lad – t' world would be crazy. Here it would start and all over would it spread; a galloping pestilence."

"But it hasn't, has it? I mean. I come from the future and I'm all right. And so's my world."

"Dost think so?" asked Gilbert, with a slight lift of the eyebrows. "Then why wert thou sent away from home?"

"That's only one thing," said Peter. But Gilbert's words struck home. Everything had changed since last night.

Gilbert continued, "There's evil in your world just as there is in this. We've had plague, pestilence: death is always with us. 'Tis with thee also; tha knows well what bad things happen each day. And 'twill not change. But what does change is how men see it. My people can bear it all – the cruelty, the plague, the cold, the starvation, and the muck – because they think that in the end 'tis worth it. And the plays tell them that. You manage to bear it as well. Why? Is it because thou art like the walking dead who do not care? Or art tha still fighting it, trying to clear the evil out while you can? I do not know and neither do you. But this I do know: that if my people think that God has left them, that all reason for living has gone, they will plant the seed of hopelessness which will make all men who come after them like toys in the face of a world they cannot control. The walking dead. Walking round in a ring while the storm rages about them. So we must stop it."

Peter listened patiently to this long speech. He didn't understand it all, but one thing he did latch on to.

"So you think I might be a zombie or something?"

"Aye, lad. Thou art if we fail."

"Thanks," murmured Peter.

"Thou art either the savior or the tiger let inside the gates. I do not know."

"Then why bring me?"

"I didn't choose thee. If you'd not been the right person to come, you'd not be here. Now remember that."

They walked for a long time without saying anything. Then Peter spoke.

"What parts will I have to act?"

"I do not know yet. I shall have to think."

The road had taken them through more densely-wooded country. At times the leaves and branches had almost obscured the sky, so they did not realize that clouds were building up all around. When they had come out of the trees and down a long, shallow slope toward the banks of the River Calder, the sun had nearly disappeared. But it was still very hot and thunder was in the air. The road, never more than a rough track, now became muddy as well. The river valley was wide and marshy, and the River Calder, broad and clear, flowed regally through it.

"Good fishing in there," said Gilbert. "It had all gone in thy day, though."

Ahead of them was a stone bridge: sturdily built and still new-looking. As the road curved, Peter could see the nine low, pointed arches and the solid stone buttresses in between each. But what took the eye most of all was a low building actually in the middle of the bridge and jutting out into the river. Peter knew little about church architecture, but even from the bank he could see that the building was something special. The detail of the intricately carved tracery work on the west front opening on to the bridge itself, the high, pointed arches of the windows and the small tower at one corner decorated with pinnacles – all these stood out sharp in the clear air, as if the mason had only just gone home with his chisel.

"The Chantry Bridge Chapel. We built it," said Gilbert.

"We?"

"The men of the town. We built the bridge and we started the chapel. The pestilence came and took many of us off, but afterwards we kept on building till 'twas finished. 'Twere started before I was born and was finished when I was still a young man, but it is mine as much as it is everyone else's who lives here. When we cross the bridge we are in Dunfield."

Peter looked beyond the bridge. He saw meadow-land where cattle grazed. Further on were a few strips of cultivated land and Peter could see the far-off figures of men bent over as they worked. Then there was more woodland – and over this could be seen, nearer and clearer now, the same skyline of huddled roofs, over-set by the soaring tower of the great church.

I've got here before the train all right, was Peter's first thought.

And we won't cross the bridge alone, was his second. For somehow – he knew not how – he was aware of someone approaching them. He turned round.

The atmosphere had been sultry, overcast, stuffy. The clouds had been gathering fast. Now at last they blotted out the sun completely: it was more like a winter's dusk than a late summer afternoon. And suddenly it was colder. Peter shivered.

The figure trudging toward them, head down and leaning on a long, heavy stick, was dressed in monkish habit, just as Peter and Gilbert were. But there all resemblance ended. The cowl was up so the head was covered. The dark, nondescript, ragged garment looked half sooty, half mildewed – in the last stages of decay. The very sight filled Peter with a curious depression – even hopelessness. We're beaten before we start, he thought. And then – why should he make me think that? There was something strange here.

Gilbert had turned as well. Stock-still he stood. His face was pale; his chin and cheekbones looked darker than ever. He said nothing.

The figure drew level. He lifted his head. Peter gasped. It was the oldest face he had ever seen. The skin was yellow with age and criss-crossed so intricately with tiny wrinkles that his eyes ached in trying to take them all in. The nose and mouth were hardly noticeable: they had almost caved into the face. The cheekbones stood out: the cheeks themselves were pulled in so that the line of the upper gums could plainly be seen. But the eyes were not old. They were large, dark, deep: they riveted Peter.

The figure spoke. The voice was high, quiet – as if coming from a million miles away. But it was very clear. "So we will enter Dunfield together."

Gilbert suddenly acted, unexpectedly and convulsively. He picked up a stone and scored the shape of a circle on the ground all round the two of them. Then he grabbed Peter by the shoulders, so that he could not get out of the circle. With his free hand he made the sign of the cross in front of his face, muttering inaudibly all the while. These actions took no more than a couple of seconds.

The ancient creature looked at them. He said no more. What might have been a smile made the hazy outline of his mouth move slightly. He lifted his hand as if in farewell and walked across the bridge. Gilbert and Peter stood watching him.

The sky grew darker. Suddenly there was a blinding flash of lightning which made Peter catch his breath with fear. The whole of the town on the hill was lit up for an instant. Almost simultaneously the thunder roared. It rolled and echoed around the shallow river valley. Then there was silence. The lonely figure ahead trudged on until it disappeared into the trees.

Gilbert spoke.

"We will go into the chapel."

They walked slowly across the bridge. Peter could hear and feel his heart racing. They reached the heavy wooden door. Gilbert opened it and Peter followed him into the cool half-light within.

As he did so, the rain at last began to fall.

– 4 –

A REHEARSAL

Inside the chapel the sound of rain on the roof could be heard. From beneath came a slight gurgling sound as the river water slopped round the base of the building and the arches of the bridge. It was cool and quiet: it was like being on a tiny island.

When his eyes were used to the half-light, Peter looked round him with surprise. The main impression was of color. The windows were glowing with it: warm blood-reds, deep greens, and blues. Between the windows the walls were covered in paintings, dark, but from which odd patches of color stood out as if they were luminous. Just inside the door was a stone font; it had a tall conical wooden cover, intricately carved and picked out in bright primary colors, with trimmings and borderings of black and gold and silver. Over the doors and many of the windows were vivid coats of arms. At the east end of the chapel, opposite the door, was a small altar, flanked by burning candles and backed by a wooden screen, again delicately carved and picked out in bright colors. And as the water of the wide river flowed outside, reflections of the colors seemed to move on the walls, the beamed wooden roof, and the stone, reed-covered floor, bare of seats or pews – so that the whole atmosphere of warm, soft radiance seemed to swim into Peter's mind.

After he had closed the door, Gilbert strode up to the altar steps and knelt down low on them, quite still.

Peter waited. The calming influence of the chapel had made disappear a lot of the fright he had felt when he saw the ancient creature. He sat down on one of the stone benches round the walls and relaxed for a few moments, waiting for Gilbert to finish. But Gilbert seemed to be taking a very long time. Peter began to feel impatient. Then he felt a little guilty, so he said the Lord's Prayer to himself quickly, out of a sense of duty. But Gilbert still didn't move. Peter wondered what on earth he could be finding to say. Now he felt merely embarrassed.

Something had to be done to pass the time, or the quiet and shade of the place would send him to sleep again. He rose and started to look at the wall paintings. They looked peculiar – odd figures of angels, devils, saints and martyrs, strange beasts and monsters. It was as if a half-mad artist had been given that great expanse of blank wall and told to doodle with his brush all over it. Then, Peter caught his breath with shock. For, quite near where he had been sitting, were three figures painted on the wall: very nearly skeletons. But not quite. Peter could not make up his mind whether he was looking at extreme old age or death. One of the figures wore nothing. But there was enough detail for Peter to realize it was a picture of a decomposing corpse. The others wore robes that were in tatters. The sight of the three figures struck chords in Peter's mind. He had seen pictures like this – though more realistic – in his own world. But another chord was being struck. What was it? Then he remembered. The figures could be direct portraits of the Ancient creature they had met at the bridge.

With an effort, Peter tore his eyes away: his fascination for the pictures seemed almost morbid. He looked again at the earlier paintings. The shock of realizing that the artist's efforts were not half-mad daubings but based on fact made him look more carefully. And now he saw a strange world in which angels and devils, life and death, laughter and solemnity, good and evil were all mixed up together.

"Now dost understand us?" said a voice in his ear. It was Gilbert.

"I don't know yet."

"The rain has stopped. We must go on."

Outside it was cooler than before. The sky was clear: the brightness of the sun made Peter blink. As they left the bridge, their feet squelched in the mud of the newly-wet track.

"Who was that old man?" asked Peter.

A moment or two passed before Gilbert answered.

"I do not know. But I am very afraid."

Silence again. Then Gilbert continued.

"Age leads to death – but there are a few to whom death does not come. We know stories about them. But too great an age leads to a living death. This is one way the fiend shows himself."

"I don't understand," said Peter.

"Nor I," said Gilbert. "But the warring parties have entered the town together."

This was the last stage of their journey. They passed the strips of cultivated land, and men stopped work to wave at them in greeting. They passed through the belt of trees and up to the gate of Dunfield itself.

"Kergate Bar," said Gilbert, as they walked under the heavy stone archway.

Once past the Bar and in the street of Kergate itself, Peter looked round him in surprise. The narrow street now was cobbled with large stones; small, black-beamed houses seemed to lean out over his head until they touched. Everything seemed dark and small. A channel ran down the middle of the street – an open sewer. It smelt. Peter held his breath.

"I told thee things were different here," said Gilbert.

"Where are we stopping?"

"At the house of Giles Doleffe. Giles is a Pageant Master – he is producing some of the plays. I have to talk to him."

Gilbert stopped in front of a house set a little apart from the rest.

"Wait here," he said, opened the door and went inside. Peter waited. A few men passed by, dressed in rough brown smocks. They took no notice of him whatever. He realized the clothes Gilbert had lent him made him merge neatly into his surroundings.

After about a minute, Gilbert came out again.

"He's at Goodybower. He's rehearsing," he said. "His children are with him."

So on they walked. They turned a corner, and there at last was the great church. Peter stopped.

"No time to look at it," said Gilbert, and hurried him on. The whole town took no more than three minutes to walk through. They soon came again to open country.

"Here's Goodybower," said Gilbert.

They were at the edge of a small, shallow quarry. Opposite them was a wall of grey rock, hacked and ridged and some ten feet tall. This wall formed one side of an auditorium with, in the middle, a wooden stage. What gave Peter most surprise was the fact that, except for what looked like two wooden buildings and three or four fairly large gaps, the rest of the arena was bounded in by quite steep raked wooden benches about six rows high – just the same as those in the travelling circus, which had, he remembered, once come to the park behind his house. Peter imagined the seats full – and for the first time he began to feel at home in this alien world, for the mental picture he received was that of a packed football crowd.

The arena was perhaps thirty yards in diameter. It was obvious anybody going to make himself heard there would have to shout.

He turned his attention to the two buildings – and saw they had wheels. He presumed therefore that they must be the "Pageants" Gilbert had spoken of. One of them was directly opposite them – the other to Peter's right. If the arena were a circle, then the two Pageants would mark off one quarter of it.

"The one nearest on the right is Heaven," said Gilbert. "The one opposite is Hell. They stay here. The other Pageants for particular plays are moved into the gaps between the seats when they are needed. That way, things are kept going."

"Hell" made Peter catch his breath: an artist with an eye for color and a talent for scaring people – or himself – must have painted it. For the mouth of Hell was a mouth indeed: like that of a monster, carefully made with yellowing, huge, sharp teeth and with streaks of painted "blood" running down them and over the gums. Wedged in between the teeth were legs, arms, heads – from that distance extremely realistic. Peter shuddered. To these people, Hell was a furious, ravening beast – and real. He remembered the paintings in the chapel and wondered if they were done by the same person.

A rehearsal of a play was going on. Two men shouted at each other in the arena; a third squatted by the side of the acting area. They turned as another voice, disembodied, called to them. Peter realized it was coming from the "Heaven" Pageant, though from where he was he could not see the speaker. At the top of the raked seating and directly opposite "Hell" sat a man watching and listening intently.

"They are rehearsing 'Cain and Abel,'" said Gilbert. "I wonder what they've done with the plough."

He looked over at the man on the seats, who in turn saw Gilbert and waved gravely.

"There's Giles," said Gilbert. "I must see him."

And he left. As he did so, the man called Giles shouted down to the actors to stop and they all, Gilbert as well, met together in the central area and talked.

Peter noticed two other people on the seating – quite near him, close to the "Heaven" Pageant and thus with their backs to him. As Gilbert walked across to Giles, they turned round to see where he had come from – and looked straight at Peter. They beckoned him to join them – and suddenly Peter felt totally scared. He was about to meet the first fifteenth-century people who had no idea who he was or where he came from. He was comforted when he had looked at them for a moment or two and had taken in their brownish smocks and stockings, their fair hair and clear skins, to realize they were children – a boy a few years older than himself, a girl a year or two younger.

"Who art thou, then?" said the boy as Peter scrambled up the raked seats. "Thou'art not from round here. Where's thi come from?"

Peter could just make out what he said. Uncle Tom and Auntie Elsie had West Riding accents – but nothing like this.

"What's thi name?" said the girl.

"Peter," said Peter, trying hard to remember the cover story Gilbert had given him. "And I was in a travelling troupe of actors from the south but they kicked me out and I was wandering round and Gilbert found me and gave me these monk's things and I'm going to watch the plays for professional interest."

All this came out in a furious rush.

"Happen tha'd better start again," said the boy.

Peter did so, and spoke very slowly. The boy and the girl listened with exaggerated care.

"From the south, tha says?" said the boy. "An actor? Tha'll be acting here, then."

"I don't know," said Peter.

"Thou shall have to change thi tooth," said the girl.

"I'll have to what?"

"Talk like us," said the boy. "I'm Francis."

"I'm Gyll," said the girl. "That's our dad talking to Gilbert. If thou'rt going to act here, tha'd better watch on."

Peter turned his attention to the actors. The little group below had broken up: Gilbert and Giles were sitting together. Cain and Abel stood on the stage. The voice from the "Heaven" Pageant sounded out again.

Cain, why art thou such a rebel
Against thy brother Abel?
To jeer at him there is no need.
If thou tithe right, thou'll get thy meed
But be thou sure if thou tithest ill
I shall repay thy great evil.

"Why, that was God speaking," cried Peter.

"Aye, course it were," said Francis. "Who else?"

Cain stood and faced the "Heaven" Pageant. He was a tall man, dark, with full lips and smouldering eyes. Peter could feel his presence – something of the "star quality" one might get from a pop singer. Cain shouted at God.

Hey, who's that hob-over-the-wall?
Who was that who piped so small?
Abel, we'll leave these perils all.
God is out of his wits.

"Eh! He shouldn't say that," gasped Gyll, in obvious horror.

"It's only a play," said Peter.

"He shouldn't say that. See what happens to him."

Cain went on.

Come on, Abel, let us go.

I know this God will be my foe;

From this place I must flit.

Cain and Abel moved down to the front of the acting area – supposing that "Hell" marked the back. Abel spoke.

Ah, brother Cain, that was ill done. His voice was calm, clear, and sorrowful. It seemed to raise Cain to fury. He ranted and screamed across the acting area.

Peter couldn't understand a single thing he said. Abel's few words by contrast were clear – little islands of sanity in the sea of roaring – but it soon became obvious that Cain was riding roughshod over him, ignoring all the cues. He was flying into a passion which seemed too real for a play. Peter saw Gilbert and Giles exchange glances: Giles rose to his feet.

Cain's voice slowed as he stooped to pick up the ragged bone left for him on the floor: the words became understandable.

I'll stop that mouth. Thou'lt smart with shame.

This cheek bone in my hand will stay

Until I've torn thy life away.

Cain lunged at Abel. But this was not the sort of fake punch that Peter had seen so often on television. Cain meant to hurt. He swung the bone at Abel with obvious force and caught him hard just above the eye as he shouted:

Now lie down there and take your rest.

To get rid of rats this way's the best.

Abel crumpled up and fell awkwardly on the ground. The skin above his right eye was split: blood poured from it.

"Well, say it, then," screamed Cain. This was obviously not part of the play. Abel was unconscious. Cain cast a look of contempt at him. He turned and shouted defiance at

Peter, at Gyll and Francis, at Gilbert and Giles, at the whole of Dunfield – and especially at the "Heaven" Pageant.

Yes, lie down there, Wretch, lie there, lie.
And if any of you think I did amiss
If he comes up here I'll do worse than this
So that all men may see.
Much worse than it is
Right so it shall be.

Peter wondered why Gilbert and Giles had not rushed up and torn Cain away from Abel as soon as the blood flowed. Now, as he looked again, he saw that they were both looking at Abel, transfixed and helpless. He turned to Francis and Gyll. They were both pale: as if they were scared out of their wits.

"'Tis Cain. He'd kill," said Francis.

"But it's only a play," said Peter once again.

Cain had stopped his raving. He stood still, listening, his nostrils twitching. For a moment everybody froze. There was complete silence. They all, Peter included, strained their ears.

Then, with a sudden wordless cry – more like a howl – Cain bounded off, up to Hell mouth itself. Inside it he went, through the back of the Pageant, awkwardly up the quarry wall and over the top, to be lost in the trees beyond.

The rest watched him go. Abel still lay motionless on the ground.

"Did you hear it? Did you hear it?" came a voice from the "Heaven" Pageant. And out of it came running an extraordinary figure in a flowing white robe, a bejewelled crown, flashing in the sunlight, and a face painted bright gold.

"'Tis God," said Gyll.

"Did you hear it?" he repeated.

The others made no answer. But Peter knew what the actor playing God meant, what had called Cain away, what had made the ears of all of them strain to hear. The trickle of blood from Abel's eye lengthened across the floor of the acting area. Gilbert's face looked deathly pale; he must have heard the sound too – the long, clear, thin note of a hunting horn.

− 5 −

THE START OF THE TASK

"See where he's going. After him," shouted Francis, and began to clatter his way down the banked wooden benches. Peter and Gyll followed hesitantly.

But Gilbert moved in front of Francis as he tried to cross the acting area, and held him by the shoulders.

"No," he said firmly.

"He'd break all your bones," said Giles. "The man's fighting mad."

"He's worse than that," said Gilbert. "Where he's running to no mortal man should be."

"What dost thou mean, Gilbert?" asked Giles.

"We'll go to thy house. I'll tell thee there. Peter, stay here. Francis and Gyll will show thee what's what."

Peter felt a little bit worried about being left by Gilbert, especially as the events of the previous few minutes had suggested that Gilbert's fears were only too true and that something strange and sinister was happening. But when he looked at Francis and Gyll he felt sure he had fallen among friends.

"So tha's not seen us plays before?" said Francis as the adults moved off.

"No, never," replied Peter.

"Ah, they're a sight, I'll tell thee," Francis continued. "And ours are the best. Better than York's, better than Lincoln's, better than Chester's. And 'tis Gilbert who makes them so."

"Do all these other places have them too, then?" asked Peter.

"Eh, where's tha been that tha doesn't know that? O' course they do."

"Ah, well," said Peter quickly. "I'm from the south, and anyway, we're always on the move."

"Well, I'm shocked, I thought you had them down there too."

Peter let the remark pass.

"Of course," said Francis. "Some places do the plays on the carts and tow them round all over the place. But yon's a daft way. We do it all in one place, with a bit of space and a bit of life to it."

"See up there," cried Gyll suddenly. They looked where she was pointing and saw three figures on the skyline hurrying round the side of the quarry; three men going the same way as Cain, to be lost to sight in the trees.

"Hey, Parkyn!" yelled Francis.

But the man took no notice.

"That Parkyn's one of them," said Francis to Gyll.

"John Horne and Jack Gibbon too," said Gyll.

"Where can they be going to?" said Francis.

"Wherever Cain has gone," said Peter. "I'm sure of that."

"Why?" said Gyll quickly, giving Peter an odd look.

"I don't know," replied Peter. Then an idea struck him. "Are they in the plays?" he asked.

"Aye," said Francis. "Parkyn and John Horne are shepherds. Jack Gibbon is Abraham. Why ask?"

50

"I don't know," said Peter. But something was nagging in his mind. The three men had run past with the same single-minded intensity shown by Cain – as if nothing on earth could stop them. The horn had called them too, thought Peter. But who had blown it? Or – he shuddered – *what* had blown it? What eyes would soon be looking at the running men? The lurid eyes of Gilbert's dream-devil? Or – and at this idea Peter felt both a slight shock of fright and the satisfaction of finding a fitting solution to a problem – the dark, deep eyes of the Ancient?

"Eh, don't worry about such carls as them," said Francis. "Come and look over here."

He led Peter to the "Hell" Pageant. Seen close to, the Pageant was a remarkable piece of work. Including the steep-sided wooden roof it was fully twenty feet high. As Peter had already noticed, the fearsome teeth of Hell mouth were the most eye-catching part.

Francis darted away, calling "Wait there" as he did so.

"I'm going up ladder at back," he cried as he disappeared from view. "Now watch," his disembodied voice called.

"Where are you?" cried Peter.

"He's in t'roof," said Gyll. "This'll shock thee," she added.

With the squeaking and creaking of rope rubbing over wood, Hell mouth actually began to open. Peter stood amazed. It had looked horrible enough before – now it was nightmarish as the teeth parted to reveal the red interior.

"Walk inside," said Gyll.

It's only painted wood, thought Peter, but even so he didn't like going in.

"Wait till we light the fires," called Gyll. "It's really Hell then. Go on in, Peter."

Unwillingly, Peter stepped past the realistic teeth, through the wooden mouth – and found himself merely in a small room, empty except for a few colored robes and some rough tools – saws and hammers – scattered about the floor. A louder straining of rope on wood came to his ears – and he saw that a system of wooden pulley-wheels and thick ropes operated the mouth, which was now closing behind him. A ladder went up through a hole in the roof – and down this ladder came Francis, smiling all over his face.

"See how it works then? Come up and try."

Peter followed Francis back up the steps, and saw that he had been turning the wooden handle of a winch, which worked the Hell mouth.

"Have a go," said Francis. "We've better than this to show thee yet."

Peter turned the handle, finding it very difficult. But through a spy-hole in the steep side of the roof, he was just able to see the great mouth satisfyingly open and close in time with his turning.

"Leave Hell mouth open and follow me," said Francis, and was gone down the ladder. Peter clambered down more awkwardly, thinking to himself that Francis was very difficult to keep up with. He followed him once again past the fearsome teeth, across the acting area, and over to Heaven. This pageant seemed built on a rather different pattern; here all the interest was above the ground level. Eight feet up was a balcony and in front of this balcony and all round it were painted stars, moons, and clouds, picked out in bright gold, silver, and white against a deep blue. From outside the effect was colorful and eye-catching: Peter had no doubt about what it was to represent. But when he went inside, he found that the sky effect was no more than a screen for an extraordinary array of gadgetry.

Francis was quick to explain.

"We can't have God and the Angels walking down ladders from Heaven to Earth. They've got to fly."

"How?" asked Peter.

"A winch up here for each one. There's a belt at the end of the rope and God or the Angel just snaps the belt round him. He stands up there on his balcony in Heaven and when he has to come down we open a trap-door, turn the handle of the winch, and let him down. When he's finished on earth, we just wind him up again."

"That sounds dangerous," said Peter.

"'Tis not. And it looks good from out there. Have a go."

"No thanks," said Peter.

"Go on. It can't hurt."

"I wouldn't dare," said Peter. But the time was not far off when he would regret not having done so.

"Suit thyself," said Francis.

"You never made all this, did you?" asked Peter.

"I helped," said Francis. "My father did most, and the carpenters and steelwrights. He's a Pageant Master. One day I'll be a Pageant Master. 'Tis best job round here. Come on, we'd best go home."

As the three of them walked on, Peter asked questions.

"Francis," he said. "Who *is* Gilbert?"

"Gilbert? Him with me Dad? He's scribe. He wrote out the copies of the plays – me Dad keeps one in t'house. And he wrote all the new plays himself."

"I know that," said Peter. "But *who* is he?"

"Well, I don't know. He lodges with us a lot of the time. Some say he used to be a priest: some say he comes from a noble family and they threw him out. No one knows and he won't say. But he's a good man, and we all get on."

"I see," said Peter. "And Cain – and those other men? Where could they run to? What's behind those trees?"

"Ah," said Gyll. "Up there's the Manor House. Beyond that's the Outwood – and there's deer and game there. Next to the Manor's the stone barn and the dovecote."

"A dovecote?" asked Peter. "One of those wooden things? What do you want doves for?"

"That's never wooden," said Francis. "Thou'rt an ignorant devil."

"Thanks," said Peter.

"'Tis stone, like the barn and the house," said Gyll. "And pigeons live in it. They nest in holes in the walls inside."

"What for?" asked Peter.

"Whee!" crowed Francis, a raucous, jeering note in his voice. "Thou'rt either mad, pig-ignorant, or been shut up in a cell all thy life."

"Don't mind him," said Gyll. "The Earl and his family at the Manor use them for meat. They can eat well all the year round."

Like a sort of medieval battery-farm, thought Peter, rather impressed. But his question was still not answered.

"So where could Cain and the others go?" he asked again.

"I know not and I'll not be bothered about such things," said Francis. "We've more to think about. There's enough wanting to act in the plays and well able to, so we won't lack for anything, even if we are without that lot."

They had re-entered the town itself by now, and were passing down the same little streets brooded over by the spire of the great church on their way back to Giles's house. As they walked, Peter felt more and more strongly that he was being watched; as if eyes were following him, never leaving him. He ignored the feeling, hoping it would go away. But it didn't – it became stronger and stronger. He turned round. There was nothing there. He walked on; then wheeled round suddenly. Was it his imagination, or had he seen a face peering round a corner for a split-second before it was withdrawn? A few more yards and they were outside Giles's house. Peter turned round suddenly again – and again he couldn't be sure that a face jerked out of sight, nor could he be sure that he heard light running footsteps fading into the distance. But he felt very suspicious.

"What's wrong with thee, then?" Francis had obviously heard nothing – and was becoming more and more sure of Peter's mental deficiency. But Gyll was quiet and looked at Peter, a slight questioning in her eyes. Peter said nothing either, but there was a nagging worry in his mind that he could not quite place.

The house they had reached was larger and set slightly apart from those surrounding it. It had two stories, unlike the rest which all had one floor only. There was a half-timbered appearance about it slightly familiar to Peter – but it was obviously new. Giles must be a man of some substance and power in the town. Yet there were no windows; merely apertures in the walls. One was closed with shutters worked from the inside – Peter supposed that the rest had them too.

Francis and Gyll opened the door and walked in; Peter followed diffidently. They walked straight in to the main room of the house, to see Giles and Gilbert sitting on the rough but sturdy wooden chairs, talking urgently in low voices. As they looked up Peter could see the flash of annoyance in their eyes at being interrupted.

Francis spoke at once. "There's Jack Gibbon, Parkyn, and John Horne gone running past Goodybower and off up the Outwood. Likely following him we saw."

Giles spoke next – his voice was deep, rich – and even broader in accent than Gilbert's had become in Peter's ears.

"Gyll and Francis, there's a job for thee. Go to every house where lives an actor in the plays. Go to every place where an actor in the plays works. Go outside the town and round all the flocks; see all the shepherds. And then come back and tell me the names of all the actors that are missing. See if any more have gone up the Outwood."

"Aye, we will. But what for?" said Francis.

"Do it," said Giles.

"You stay here, Peter," said Gilbert.

Francis and Gyll clattered out of the house without another word. There was silence for a while, as Giles looked at Peter curiously.

"He knows all about thee," said Gilbert. "He knows where thou art from and why."

"So what's to be done?" said Giles.

"He'll have to be put in the plays," said Gilbert.

"Which ones?" said Giles.

"Aye, that's the devil of it," said Gilbert.

Peter found himself talking quickly. "Those men who ran off," he said. "There was Cain: we all saw him. And Francis told me the others were Abraham and two of the shepherds."

"Aye, 'twere them I told thee of in the train," said Gilbert.

"I think they've gone off to see someone – whoever it is who's doing all this. He's called them to him. He's giving his orders."

Giles and Gilbert exchanged glances.

"So I ought to be in the plays they're in because they know what's going to happen," said Peter.

"He is right," said Gilbert.

"I can put him in those plays," said Giles. "They are all plays I produce. I doubt if Abel will be fit – though if he is I'll never talk him out of acting. The lad playing Isaac is a useless lump; I said I would have him out of it if I could find a better – now I have. The third shepherd will be angry – but he's young and he can do it next year. I'll see him."

"But what's special about those plays?" asked Peter. "Why should I be in them and no others?"

"Aye, that's odd," said Giles.

"There might be others yet," said Gilbert. "And look, 'tis not really forty-odd little plays we do; 'tis one big play."

"So?" said Giles.

"So if one play is altered: if one play finishes in the opposite way that it should, then the rest will *mean* something different."

"What art thou driving at, Gilbert? ''Tis beyond me, I'll tell thee," said Giles.

"If God does not stop Abraham from killing Isaac, it means that all the plays that follow are telling a different story. The Abraham and Isaac Play says that God is with us. What if it says straight out that God is not with us?"

"All right," said Giles. "What about the other plays?"

"If Cain gets away with murder," said Gilbert, "nothing that follows can be taken seriously. But Noah and his family cannot be drowned in the flood because that would mean that no more plays could be done: there would be no people left on earth. So that play will go on as it is written."

"I don't see it," said Giles. "But I'll believe thee since there's naught else I can believe. What about the Shepherd's Play? If something's to go awry in that, what is it to be. Tha's been telling me all that happens in it was made up by thee."

"I must think," said Gilbert.

Peter was trying to remember what Gilbert had said before. It came back with difficulty.

"In the train," he said, and noticed Giles looking mystified as he did so, "you said that you couldn't let men who had just hanged a man go to the cradle. And then you said that in your dream the shepherds looked for Jesus and didn't find him. What did you mean?"

"Aye, that's it," said Gilbert. "What happened in my dream? I cannot see it clearly. If the shepherds hanged Mak they would be murderers."

"Nay, Gilbert. That's daft talk. Sheep-stealers should be hanged. Tha's right soft in that play," said Giles. "I could make a good hanging for thee, and tha'll not let me. 'Tis a good chance missed."

"An eye for an eye and a tooth for a tooth? Is that the sort of world thou seest, Giles Doleffe?" cried Gilbert.

"What else?" said Giles.

"God damn thee, man," shouted Gilbert. "'Tis all wasted on thee and the likes of thee."

Peter looked from one to the other in horror. Surely even these two were not to be split apart?

"I'll not produce a play," said Giles with heavy emphasis, "that teaches men to be soft on them as steals sheep. If a man has his sheep stolen, then the thief has killed him, as sure as if he had put a knife between his ribs."

"I know," said Gilbert. "But I want men to look beyond that. The shepherds will not hang Mak: they toss him up in a blanket. They have their sheep back – and they forgive him."

"But he'll do it again," said Giles.

"What do we do these plays for?" insisted Gilbert. "Tha'll never tell me tha'd go into church as large as life just after tha'd killed a man?"

Giles thought a moment.

"Aye," he said finally. "To get it off my chest. To be forgiven."

"Aye, tha'd need to be forgiven as well as the shepherds."

"But," said Peter. "If Mak gets hanged by the shepherds, and then they see the child in the manger, it won't mean anything because they are guilty of murder."

"Aye, blood on their hands," said Gilbert. "It will mean Christ does not forgive."

"But if the cradle is empty, then there can't be any more plays because there will be no Jesus," said Peter.

58

"Thou hast a sharp mind, Peter," said Gilbert. "And 'tis there I'm stuck, because I've no notion what will happen. I must think on."

"And so must Peter," said Giles. "For now the real work begins."

"What work?" said Peter.

"In two days thou'lt be acting in the plays: thou'lt be Abel, Isaac, and Daw, the third shepherd. So far, thou knows not a word of them. It will be hard for thee – but it must be done."

I'm not looking forward to this, thought Peter.

"Thy head will be pounding before we have finished," said Giles. "I'll show thee how to do it while Gilbert thinks out why. Now, there's no time to be lost."

And that was how Peter started on the hardest and most frustrating task of his life.

– 6 –

PETER AND THE PLAYS

The beginning of it was postponed, however. From a door at one side of the room appeared a small cheerful woman carrying a wooden tray.

"'Tis the wife, Peter," said Giles. "This is Peter, my love. A boy actor from the south."

"I heard different through the door," said Giles's wife. "But I cannot be surprised by owt I hear in this place. Tha's had a longer journey than most, I'd say. So sup up with this."

There were some still-hot oat cakes on the tray and pewter mugs full of beer. Gilbert and Giles reached for the cakes and ale at once.

"Healey Ale. The best," said Gilbert, swigging noisily.

Peter quite enjoyed the oat cakes, though they were strong and somehow chewy. One sip of the beer, however, made him realize it was far different from the Double Diamond his father had allowed him a quick swallow of the previous Christmas; very dark, heavy, and bitter.

"I don't think I want this," he said.

"I'll drink it," said Giles – just, Peter thought, beating Gilbert to it. "Fetch the lad some milk."

The milk, too, when it came, tasted strong and sour: Peter gave an involuntary heave at the first mouthful. But he soldiered on till it was finished. After all, he thought, if I don't keep it down I'm going to starve. So I'd better get used to it.

He was helped, of course, by the fact that his last food had been a packet of sandwiches eaten just north of Sandy: he could have swallowed a horse.

For a while nobody spoke. The shadows outside were beginning to lengthen as the evening wore on. The realization of hunger brought Peter to the realization of tiredness as well: his sleep behind the bush earlier in the afternoon now seemed no more than a quick doze which had just about kept him going. But Giles was not going to let him get away so easily. As soon as the meal was finished and his wife had taken the things away, he spoke.

"Thou'lt have to do some work tonight. Tha knows nowt about the plays at all: there'll be a lot of time saved tomorrow if thou canst get some idea tonight and sleep on them. Canst tha read?"

"Of course I can read," said Peter, rather offended.

"There's a shock coming, Peter," said Gilbert, smiling to himself.

Giles had opened a large cupboard and brought out the manuscript, a bound book, with pages of parchment, in size about a foot by eight inches. It was new: as Peter turned the pages over he was struck once again by these people's love of color. He stopped at one page and looked at it in more detail.

PROCESSUS NOE CUM FILIIS DUNFELD

NOE

Myghtfull God veray, maker of all that is,
Thre persons withoutten nay, oone God in endles blis.

And so on.

Peter looked at it in horror. At first he could make nothing of the writing at all. When he had begun to fathom out a few letters he realized the words meant virtually nothing to him either. He remembered one of his teacher's oft-repeated jokes: "The dawn of legibility in his handwriting has revealed his utter inability to spell." A feeling of hopelessness, not for the first time in the six hours he had been in this strange world, spread through him.

"Canst read now, lad?" smiled Gilbert.

Again, and not for the first time, Peter turned on him.

"You knew this, didn't you?" he stormed. "I can't understand a single rotten word of it. How do you expect me to learn it?"

"We'll manage," said Gilbert.

At that moment, Francis and Gyll came back. Peter forgot his anger for a moment.

"We've been everywhere," said Francis.

"Round all the booths in Market Street," said Gyll.

"To the weavers, the glovers, the dyers, the nail-makers, the lot," said Francis.

"We've been all up t'moors over Horbury looking for sheep and shepherds," said Gyll.

"And there's no one else gone. Not a soul," said Francis.

"You've done well. The task is lighter than we thought," said Giles. "Go through to your mother and have a bite to eat – then come back here. There's more work for thee now if Master Peter is to learn his parts."

"Aye, Peter," said Gilbert. "We'll manage well enough, just as I said, when they're back from eating."

"How?" said Peter, who felt his annoyance returning.

"Thou'lt see," said Gilbert, and would have said more if there had not been a knock on the outside door.

"Who can that be?" said Giles, not stirring.

"Best look," said Gilbert. "It's thy house."

"Aye, wife and children still eating," said Giles and went unwillingly to the door.

"Well?" he said as he opened it.

"'Tis I, Master Giles," said the voice of a young man. Peter could see a head of fair hair and a fresh-complexioned face – also a livid and still fresh scar above the right eye. It was Abel.

"Come in, lad," said Giles. "What's with thee, then?"

"I'm all right, Master Giles. Don't put me out of t'play: I'll do the part. I've only a throbbing head; I'll be well by Corpus Christi."

"Aren't you afraid?" said Gilbert.

"What of?" said Abel.

"Thy brother," said Gilbert.

"Why should I be afraid of him?" said Abel.

"He tried to kill thee at t'rehearsal. And it wasn't the first time. He'll have thee for sure on the day," said Gilbert.

"Not he," said Abel. "He gets excited, that's all; he loves the plays, tha knows. He'd not hurt a soul."

"But he's hurt thee, lad," said Giles.

"Aye, that's true," said Abel.

"So I ought not to let thee act," said Giles.

"Daft," said Abel. "I know my own brother: none knows him better. He's big, but he's gentle. He'll not hurt me."

"Dost tha still know him?" said Gilbert.

"What dost tha mean?" said Abel.

"Has he changed in the last weeks?" said Gilbert.

"Aye, o'course he has. He's going to be in the plays. So he's nervous-like. 'Tis all t'same to me – but he worries about it," said Abel.

"And that's all there is to see?" said Gilbert.

"O' course," said Abel. "What else is there? And what's it to thee?"

"I'll not have thee in t' plays, for thy own sake, lad," said Giles, with heavy finality.

"Now look here, Master Giles," said Abel. "I came here in a good humor. I thought tha'd be pleased I was all right. Instead tha tries to stop me being in them at all. Why? Tha said I were right good in t'part before, and I've spent a lot of time on it; 'tis a big thing for me, getting in t' plays. And what art tha saying daft things about my brother for? Art tha trying to make an excuse out of him so I'll not know you think I'm no good? I'm offended, Master Giles. You've vexed me, you have. I wouldn't act for thee now if . . ."

"I'm sorry," said Giles, cutting in to Abel's speech. "O' course I'll let thee act if that's how you feel. Nobody could do the part like thee: it could have been written for thee."

"It was," said Gilbert.

"But all I say is, watch out. Take care of thyself. It could happen again and next time you might get thumped worse."

"Never," said Abel. "There's a lot of fuss here about nowt. I'll leave thee to it then."

And off he went.

"One play less for Peter," said Giles when he had gone.

"I don't like it," said Gilbert. "We must take good care of him: never let him out of our sight when the play is on."

Francis and Gyll had re-entered the room: their mother accompanied them and sat down with them, a smile of radiant good nature on her face.

"There's only two plays for thee to learn if Abel's all right," said Giles. "So we'll all sit round and read them to thee. Abraham first: I'll read Abraham; Gilbert be God; Francis, you be Isaac, while Gyll and the wife be the servants. Gyll, read the angel when the time comes. We'll share the book – though I should think we'd know it off by heart."

So they read, and Peter listened intently. He had already noticed the plays were written in verse; it did not seem at all odd to him. It also occurred to him that Giles had been asking a serious question when he had asked him if he could read – people who couldn't read could learn verse easily while prose would defeat them.

Giles read Abraham's first speech gravely, calling on God for help at the end of a long and disappointing life –

Lord, when shall Death take me in thrall?
For a hundred years I've walked these ways.
Oh Lord, soon now I hope death shall –
It's time he held me in his gaze.

Then Giles as God spoke out to Abraham, giving the orders to sacrifice – and then Francis's voice was heard, reading the part of Isaac. Peter now listened even more carefully as Isaac professed his love for his father who was already resolved to kill him. Peter had read the Abraham and Isaac story in the Bible: he knew more or less what happened. But to hear the rough voice of Francis reading the part and to realize that soon these words would have to be possessed by heart made him react with something stronger than his previous bored indifference. As he listened he began to fit the story to himself and his thoughts began to wing away back to his own century. With an effort he resumed attention.

Isaac now knew he was to die.

When I am dead and covered in clay, who then will be your son? the voice of Francis asked.

Ah, Lord, that I should see this day, said Abraham.

For I have been the only one, said Isaac.

Peter still listened intently. Francis as Isaac continued and Giles as Abraham answered.

The shining of your silver blade,
It makes me fear much more to die.

Giles's voice was grave.

On your face you shall be laid,
So when I strike you shall not see.

I've got to do that, thought Peter, and a flash of unwilling fear shot over him – just as it had when Francis had tried to make him walk through Hell mouth. The voice of God and the coming of the Angel seemed very long delayed: the feeling of alarm in Peter persisted as he thought what might happen if Gilbert were right and something or someone was out to wreck the plays. And he was, after all, sure that Gilbert was right. He began to understand what he meant – what this credulous audience would be feeling if they had first of all seen Cain get away, literally, with murder and then Isaac killed because there was no one to save him. And he began to think of the Abraham he was to act with, whom he had already seen running hell-for-leather to a destination best not thought of; possibly by now programmed to kill. After all, if the Angel had not arrived, the real Isaac would have been killed.

They had finished.

"Well, Peter," said Giles's wife. "What didst think?"

"Very good," said Peter. "But I'll never learn it in time."

"That tha wilt," said Giles. "We know it by heart: we will do it again and this time you'll follow in the book. See now if thou canst make sense of the words."

Through the play they went again; Peter, now knowing more or less what to expect, found that he was beginning to make a little sense of the writing.

Perhaps, he thought, it was not such an impossible task after all.

"Right," said Giles when they had finished. "Shepherds now. Gilbert, thou'lt be Coll, the old one. Francis, read Gyb, the middle one. Gyll, read Daw – that's the young one Peter will be acting on Corpus Christi Day. I'll read Mak and my wife here will be my wife in the play."

"Her name's Gyll, like mine," said Gyll, rather proudly, Peter thought.

"Now, Peter, listen well here," said Giles. "Tha's got to have thy wits about thee in this."

"All right," said Peter, and listened as Gilbert read the first speech of Coll, the first shepherd, complaining of his lot.

Lord, these weathers are cold and I am ill-happed.
I'm nearly dead, so long have I napped.
My legs fold up, my fingers are chapped.
This is not as I would, for I am all lapped
In sorrow.
In storms and tempest,
Now in the east, now in the west,
Woe is him who has never rest
Midday or tomorrow.

A long catalogue of ills followed. Is moaning all he can do? thought Peter. But what Coll had to say was nothing to the diatribe about married life put forward by Gyb, the second shepherd, when he entered.

These men that are wedded don't get their own will.
Not a bit! Instead their tongues they keep still.
God knows they get led right hard and full ill.
Not awake or in bed do they get their fill.
By this tide,
My lesson I've learned.
My part I've found
But the man who gets bound
Just has to abide.

Daw, the young shepherd, as read by Gyll, seemed a cheeky lad, resentful of the fact that he felt he was, as the young apprentice, not treated fairly by the two older men.

We're wet and we're weary while our master winks
But they're always late, are the food and the drinks
For our victuals.
Both the dame and the sire.

When we're run in the mire.
Cut down on our hire
And pay us so little.

I like him, thought Peter.

It was the character of Mak who was really interesting. Giles's deep, sonorous voice sounded very impressive: his delivery and understanding of what he was reading made Peter feel that a creation of great interest was unfolding before him as the reading progressed. For first of all was the idea that Mak was to be suspected of thievery: then to be feared as something unknown. Then, Peter thought, why should he be feared? He's a man like the rest of them: he has a rotten time at home, just like poor old Gyb. After all, what was Mak saying about his wife now?

     . . . She's sprawled out by the fire –
In a house full of children. She drinks well, too,
Though that's the only good thing she can do, I fear.

Still, the fact remained that the shepherds feared Mak was a sheep-stealer; which was an unforgiveable thing to be even if he did have to live as well.

But what was this? The shepherds prepared for sleep and Mak prepared for thieving. And Mak pretended to cast a spell round the shepherds.

Cast about you a circle as round as the moon.
So I can do as I like, till it's noon.
Now lie there, you shepherds, as still as a stone
Under the power of the spell that I moan
Over you.
Over your heads my hands I lift.
Out go your eyes: out goes your sight.
Now, that's enough. I have to shift
With my job to do.

But was he pretending? Peter cast his mind back to what Gilbert had said about the superstition of these people – and that they accepted what they saw before them. Was Mak then a magician? How could he be accepted, let alone understood? Was he not, in fact, a very frightening creature, in spite of his good humor, making jokes out of his lot and his evil-doing?

Anyway, by this time Mak had stolen the sheep and taken it back to his house. The homely tones of Giles's wife now sounded as she and Mak cooked up a scheme to hide the sheep. Mak would go back to the shepherds and wake up as if he had been there all the time. He would say he had dreamt that his wife had had yet another baby and that he had to get back home as quickly as he could. Meanwhile, his wife would put the sheep in the cradle and pretend it was the baby when the shepherds came round looking – as both agreed they surely would.

And that was exactly what happened. Mak stole back, woke up, went home, all unsuspected – except, Peter noticed, by Daw, the young one. For Daw had a dream as well – of Mak!

I thought he was dressed in a wolf-skin.

Coll, the oldest shepherd, scoffed at this, but Daw went on.

While we were asleep, I dreamt that he rose
And trapped a fat sheep – but he made no noise.

He's got more sense, that Daw, than the rest of them put together, thought Peter with satisfaction.

Soon the shepherds discovered that they really had lost one of their flock – a ram. So round they went to Mak's house. Mak was singing; Gyll was groaning; the shepherds took no notice and searched the place. Mak and his wife were righteously indignant. Pointing to the cradle, Mak said,

And as I'm true and loyal to God above, I pray
That if I lie, may this be my first meal today.

And Gyll was equally insistent.

I pray to God so mild
If ever I you beguiled
I'll eat this very child
That lies in the cradle.

Those shepherds will never believe that rubbish, thought Peter. But he was wrong: they left the house and Mak and Gyll seemed safe. But Gilbert knew his job as a playwright. Even as the shepherds gathered outside the house ready to carry on the search, the plot moved on. For old Coll asked a simple question:

Gave ye the child anything?

Of course they hadn't. So back went Daw, and the two older shepherds followed him. This time they insisted on seeing the baby if they were going to give him some money. So, in spite of Mak's undoubted fury, Daw forced his way to the cradle.

Let me give him a kiss. I'll lift up the clout.
What the devil is this. He's got a great long snout.

Coll, of course, insisted it was a birthmark, but Gyb recognized it at once. So Mak's scheme had failed.

As Daw, presumably, took the young ram out of the cradle, he said,

Will you see how they swaddle
His four feet in the middle?
I never saw in a cradle
A hornèd lad before.

That's odd, thought Peter. You might almost think a lad with horns was the devil himself. And then another idea struck him. The shepherds would soon be going to another cradle: the very opposite of the devil would be in that one. Was this what Gilbert was trying to do in telling the story of Mak – to see how the shepherds dealt with the threat to their lives that Mak posed before he allowed them to continue to the cradle in which Christ was? For now, of course, the point of the play had been reached that Gilbert and Giles had previously argued over. Peter noticed that Coll and Gyb, the old shepherds, were for hanging and burning Mak and Gyll; it was young Daw who suggested tossing them up in a blanket.

Then the angel spoke, the shepherds went to the cradle, each presented a gift, Mary blessed them and the play was over. Peter clapped.

"So tha liked it," said Giles.

"Oh, yes," said Peter. "But I'd like to follow it in the book, if I could."

"Of course," said Gilbert. "We'll do it from memory again."

It was getting steadily darker: Peter had to take the book over to one of the open shutters to make much out of what was written. Even before the play was over, he felt his eyes closing of their own accord: even before the angel had appeared to the shepherds, Gilbert had motioned to the others to stop.

"The lad's had a long day: the longest of his life. 'Tis time to stop: the plays will still be here in the morning."

– 7 –

DIFFICULTIES

Peter was given a greyish woollen nightshirt and a surprisingly comfortable straw mattress with three woollen blankets of great thickness. It was a warm night and he slept in the main room under the window which opened out over the street. Gilbert and Francis slept in this room as well; Francis on the opposite side of the room, Gilbert by the door, as if on guard. Giles, his wife, and Gyll disappeared up on to the upper floor.

It did not take Peter long to go to sleep. For a few minutes he lay trying to sort out the jumble of memories this amazing day had given him. Before he finally surrendered himself to sleep he was left with four questions in his mind. Would he be able to learn these parts and act them convincingly? Would he get back into his own time when it was all over? What secret lay behind the missing actors and the Ancient? – and, coupled with this, had someone really been following and watching him all the way back from Goodybower to Giles's house?

There was no time to work out answers to these questions. Sleep came but it was not restful. There were long, fitful periods when Peter did not know if he were awake or asleep. Disconnected fragments of the words of the plays – such as he could remember – ran chasing round his mind; somehow they got mixed up with the hurrying rhythm of a train at speed; once or twice Peter could hear nothing but the noise of a train and could feel its lively rocking motion. He felt that with only a little effort of will he could make himself wake up in his own century. But before he could try, the sensations disappeared and he was firmly back in medieval Dunfield. And this went on for hours, Peter tossing and turning feverishly, until a dark and dreamless sleep finally took him.

It must have been about three o'clock in the morning that Peter suddenly found himself awake, every nerve astrain. The rough wool of the blankets Giles had given him scratched his chin. His eyes tried to pierce the darkness; his ears were alert for the smallest sound. He was instinctively aware of danger. But what had woken him up?

He grew gradually used to the darkness so that first he saw faint streaks of light through the cracks in the shutters; then he was able to make out the shape of the shutters themselves. But there was nothing to see that was suspicious. Deep rumbling snores came from the direction of the door where Gilbert was sleeping – dreamlessly, Peter hoped. Lighter breathing came from where Francis slept. Nothing seemed amiss inside the room: that much was certain.

Peter then tried to concentrate as hard as he could on sounds outside. Soon he was hardly aware of the snoring from inside the room. He strained his ears till his head ached. And then he was rewarded. He heard something.

It was the light tap of footsteps outside: leather sandals on cobblestones. Peter concentrated even harder. He could not make out how many people were there; but he was sure there was more than one.

The footsteps grew louder; then they stopped – right out-side the door. Gilbert snored and muttered in his sleep; Peter thought he could hear murmuring outside: low voices in conversation. Then the footsteps started again and Peter relaxed.

But for no more than two seconds. The footsteps stopped – right outside his window. Peter was aghast. The mutter-ing started again: whoever it was now stood only two feet away, separated from him by a wattle and daub wall. No words could be made out, but the tone was of secretive urgency.

Then the talking stopped. A few seconds of silence, and then – scratch, scratch. Someone or something was fid-dling with the shutters. The scratches gave way to creaks – whoever it was had now started to force them. Paralyzed with fright, Peter strained his eyes staring at the shutters, and was convinced he saw something – it might have been the blade of a knife – poking through the crack down the middle where the two shutters met. The something jerked sharply a few times, making splintering sounds. On its up-ward jerks it fetched up against the beam laid across the in-side of the shutters to keep them closed. So they held firm. After what seemed hours, the blade disappeared. The voices started again: then so did the footsteps, and both died away.

Peter lay back in his bed, his heart racing. For a while he was too frightened to think. Then he debated with him-self whether to wake the others. But what could he tell them? For all he knew this happened every night in medieval Eng-land: perhaps the watchmen on their rounds had orders to test all the shutters from outside. And he was certainly not going to give Francis cause to think him any dafter than he did already.

Before he had made his mind up, however, he was asleep again, and this time he slept without interruption until he was woken up by the full glare of the sun shining through the window, for the shutters had already been opened.

"Come on, Peter lad," said Giles, who had just opened them. "Half the day is gone and not a scrap of work done."

Peter sprang out of bed, pulled his clothes on, and rushed out into the scullery to swill his face and chest in a bowl of cold water. There was breakfast – more oat cakes and milk – and then Giles spoke.

"This morning I shall try to help thee learn the words. This afternoon we shall walk through the plays. We shall have a good idea of what sort of performance it is by nightfall."

I bet you will, thought Peter. And it will be a rotten one, I can tell you now. Because though, since last night, he had now some idea of what the plays were about, the task ahead depressed him enormously.

As the morning went on, the feeling of depression increased. The next four hours were hard and frustrating. Giles and Peter were in the front room alone: Giles's wife worked in the scullery at the back. Gilbert, Francis, and Gyll had been up early and disappeared long before Peter was awake, because, as Giles pointed out, there was so much work to do at Goodybower, and besides, it would make many people very suspicious if they all disappeared just before Corpus Christi. Peter felt lonely and very much in uncharted waters.

Outside, the day was superb. A hot sun shone out of a cloudless sky. All the sounds of a busy day in the little town drifted in through the window – footsteps, the cries and shouts of vendors calling their wares from the booths in nearby Market Street, the rumble of carts, and the clack of the hooves of horses and donkeys. At intervals came the sound of bells from the tower of the great church. When Peter could steal a glance outside, he saw the shapes of the buildings and trees standing out clear and sharp against the blue sky, as if they were all brand new. And up and down the street passed people with their goods, their carts, their animals, intent on living their own lives. Outside was hurrying, scurrying life that Peter would dearly have loved to investigate. Inside were the words of plays which, by comparison, seemed meaningless – and a teacher who was a hard task-master, demanding, impatient, and fast becoming openly contemptuous.

Some of the time Peter tried to pick his way through the written script: but this was still very difficult. Mostly he was forced over and over again to repeat what Giles said as he declaimed two or three lines at a time. If Peter burbled them out in a rush immediately Giles stopped, while they were still in his mind, he was more or less accurate: if he tried to say them again, more slowly, they had gone. When he did manage to master a few lines he felt a huge relief, soon to go when he found he forgot them as soon as he had learnt a few more. Meanwhile Giles was becoming more and more short-tempered with him.

"Thick. Thick, thou art," he burst out once. "That Gilbert could have all to choose from and yet pick thee – by heck, I grieve at it."

Peter wondered whether Giles or Francis thought he was the more stupid. He knew neither of them thought much of him.

The morning wore on. The parts of Isaac and Daw, the young shepherd, had no rhyme or reason at all now for Peter. If he could find a way just to run through enough of the words to pass muster he could be thankful. But Giles, as well as being bad-tempered, was a perfectionist.

"I'll get these words in thy brain even if I have to bore a hole and shove them in," he said in disgust. Peter felt humiliated. The plays to him were now no more than a garbled mess.

When Gilbert, Francis, and Gyll came in, Francis covered in sawdust and telling everybody of the throne he had been building for Caiaphas the High Priest, Peter felt too miserable to take any notice. Even the herb-smelling stew Giles's wife had made for them all and the crusty bread that went with it could not revive his spirits. For he knew well that they had all come from Goodybower expecting an afternoon going through the plays so that he could put the words he had learnt into place and thus show himself up to the task he had been brought here for. And he wasn't up to it at all. He was completely inadequate.

The afternoon showed it. The rehearsal was a total disaster. Such words as he could remember came out in the wrong order. He had not mastered any of the cues so that he never knew when to come in with his speeches. The night before, when listening to the others, he had been moved by the conversation between Abraham and Isaac. Now he was trying to be Isaac it sounded complete nonsense – and it was, because when he answered Gilbert (reading Abraham) at all, he was always grotesquely wrong. When, after complete confusion, Giles suggested they cut their losses and have a go at the Shepherds' Play, Peter's relief was short-lived. It took him only a minute or two to lose his way in that too.

What made it all worse was that Giles was trying to give Peter some idea of his movements on the stage. After a few minutes of being pushed around the room from one to another, Peter was ready to give up. But Gilbert came to his rescue.

"Giles, how can he see where to go if he does not know the words?"

"Give him the book, then," said Giles disgustedly. "That may sort him out."

But it didn't. It didn't help in the least. Where before he had cudgelled his brains to remember, now he strained his eyes to see and understand. He saw Gilbert's eyes clouded over with doubt.

He thinks I've let him down, thought Peter. He's wondering why he brought me. If it comes to that, so am I.

"Hopeless," said Giles, after what seemed ages of long-drawn out embarrassment. "By God, I'll put him through it tomorrow."

Peter could see Francis nearly doubled up with silent laughter. But Gyll was looking at him strangely, with a mixture of puzzlement and sympathy.

"He's had enough," said Gilbert. "We are asking too much. Give him a rest. Let him sleep on it."

"By God, he slept on it last night," shouted Giles. "He can go to sleep for ever for aught I care. There's tomorrow for learning and rehearsing, the next day for the procession, and then he's on. Hopeless. Hopeless it is. Best put Francis on if we must make a change. Not this fool."

"If he was not meant to be here, he would not be here," said Gilbert firmly.

"Say that again," said Giles, "and I will ask for proof."

All I've managed to do, thought Peter, is to split up two friends. And as they continued arguing among themselves, wearisomely going over the same points again and again, his confusion and misery grew and grew. Nobody spoke to him. He refused the oat cakes a shamefaced Gyll offered him.

"I couldn't eat them," he said to her. "They would choke me."

"I know," she said, and turned away to her mother.

He felt really lonely now: the sensation of being marooned returned that he had experienced when he had first arrived in this strange century.

The evening drew on, the curfew rang, noise on the streets outside died away, dusk approached. The argument simmered down and a frigid silence took its place. It was the sort of atmosphere you could cut with a knife. Giles and Gilbert sat apart, each moodily staring into his jar of ale. Francis whittled away at a stick. Gyll and her mother had disappeared to the back of the house.

Francis broke the silence.

"Here, Peter," he said. "Catch this."

And he threw something at him. Peter didn't catch it: he had to grope for it on the floor. It was a little wooden pipe – like a roughly made flageolet. The center of the stick was hollowed out, holes were made in it, and the little mouthpiece was neatly carved. It was a craftsman's throwaway doodle, and he admired it tremendously.

"I've made myself one," Francis said. "Let's give them a tune."

He started to play. Peter gingerly blew down his and heard its piercing note. He stopped up the holes with his fingers – and found it really played.

Between them they improvised a sort of shambling duet and Peter felt himself warming once again to Francis. But Giles interrupted them.

"Shut that noise," he shouted. "'Tis not right that this goes on so late; a gut-griping row like that. 'Tis time we slept."

It was too dark now for Peter to see what sort of expression was on Francis's face – but he was sure it would be angry. Though slightly guilty at being the cause of friction between Francis and his father, he couldn't help feeling cheered up at the fact that someone at least was not completely against him – especially when that person had seemed like an enemy before.

Very soon they prepared themselves for bed. Gilbert did not say a word. After his prayers he went straight to sleep, as if he were too sick to have anything to do with any of them.

But for a few minutes Francis talked to Peter.

"There's something odd about thee," he said. "But I'll not ask thee what it is. Yesterday, I thought you were daft, as well as a Southerner and soft."

He thought for a moment or so, and it was on the tip of Peter's tongue to tell him more about himself. But Francis went on.

"You may be daft: you didn't do so well today. But Gilbert doesn't think you are. And if he says you're not, then you're not. And you may be a Southerner – but you're not soft. You stood up well to me Dad today."

Now Peter did speak.

"Why does he want to make me look a fool all the time?"

"He does not. That's just his way. You'll see why soon. You may thank him for it."

"I doubt it," said Peter.

"But there's not much time left," said Francis. "The parts will have to be learnt."

"I'll never do it," said Peter, and the short-lived pleasure of this conversation died away as the misery of his task came back to him.

"You'll see," said Francis. "Now get to sleep. You'll need to. But you can cheer up. I mean that. You'll see."

80

– 8 –

A DEATH'S-HEAD IN THE DARK

Francis finished talking. Peter had only time for one thought before he was asleep – that he had said nothing about the attempt the night before to open the shutter of his window.

It was the dark sleep of exhaustion that descended on him. But, as on the previous night, it was to be interrupted. Just as before, some time in the dead, small hours, Peter jerked awake, every nerve alert. This time he must have slept through the footsteps and whispering – it was a definite and very strange noise that had disturbed him. It was the splintering sound of splitting wood, yet there was something rhythmic about it. It's like a brace and bit, he thought.

Suddenly he realized that was exactly what it was. There was a louder splintering noise, then silence – then a shower of dust and slivers of wood on the bed and the moonlight pouring through the perfectly round hole in the shutter, just like the beam from the projection-box at the pictures.

Peter watched, fascinated and powerless to speak – completely mystified.

The beam of light started to fluctuate in size, as if something was being poked through the hole. There was a sound of wood against wood – and then at last Peter realized what was happening. The hole was drilled just under the board holding the shutters closed: the board was being removed; pushed up and over the brackets on to the bed. Awkwardly it fell, just missing Peter's leg.

What happened next took only a split-second, and was done before he could cry out a warning to the sleeping household. The shutters were pushed open, two long arms of huge strength descended – one pushed a ball of rough woollen cloth in Peter's mouth, the other gripped him round the shoulders and hauled him out of the bed, through the shutters and into the road outside as if he had been no more than a sack of straw. Whoever it was had pulled out one of the blankets as well; Peter was smothered in it uncomfortably, so that he could see nothing. However, it kept him warmer than the nightshirt on its own would have done.

He was half carried, half hustled along, bruisingly and so quickly his feet hardly touched the ground. His captors said nothing: all he could hear faintly through the blanket was the sound of sandalled feet on stone. Soon that changed: they were on grass and so, presumably, out of the town.

After a few minutes Peter began to feel he was going to suffocate. The blanket was thick and rough: it was held tightly round him. He couldn't breathe, he felt dizzy; he didn't know whether he was right way up or upside down, conscious or unconscious. He must have blacked out.

He opened his eyes to a sight he could make nothing of at all. At first he only registered a faint light and many shadows. Then he realized that the light came from two candle-lanterns in front of him. Behind the lanterns were the dark shapes of men standing. Behind them were more shadows still. Above and round about was blackness. It was cold: Peter now had only his nightshirt on. There was almost no sound – but what sound came was the oddest thing of all;

an occasional, quiet noise, half like a high-pitched chuckle, half like bubbling. It was odd yet familiar. He had heard it before many times, he was sure. But he could not place it.

Nobody spoke. He wondered if he had just been dumped in front of a line of statues. As his eyes grew used to the candlelight, he saw they were in what seemed like a large hall. There was straw on the ground and a strong, sour smell, the sort his father, with a wrinkle of the nose, would have called "definitely agricultural." And, by straining his eyes to the limit, he could make out the walls, which again were peculiar; it looked as if there were rows and rows of even darker holes in the darkness of the stone.

He looked again at the human figures. There were five standing motionless in front of him. The candles flickered: their shadows stretched behind them and moved. Peter felt for a moment that they were not shadows but more men. The feeling passed – but it came back again more than once in the next minutes.

The silence was broken.

"So I see you again, Peter," said a voice, quiet, cold, high, and from a million miles away.

One of the figures moved forward. It was hooded, dark, a mere silhouette even though the candles were shining on it. As it moved forward the candles flickered wildly and nearly went out. A coldness touched Peter – and for a split-second he was back at his own house, in the kitchen and opening the refrigerator door.

"Once again," the voice said.

It was the Ancient.

"But here our ways must part," the high, quiet voice went on. "Stay here. Wait here, in the dark. And soon your gap in time will arrive. You will go home, to the place you never should have come from."

"Who are you?" said Peter.

"You never should have come," the voice persisted.

Once again there was the odd bubbling sound.

"You should have stayed, so that our will could have its way," said the Ancient.

"I didn't ask to come," said Peter.

"No," said the Ancient. "That meddling playwright should not have gone to get you."

"He didn't ask to, either," said Peter.

"No," said the Ancient.

There was a silence. Peter felt obscurely that he had scored a point. Though he was sorely frightened, he had managed to speak up for himself – now he felt a little surge of confidence.

But then the Ancient figure bent, picked up one of the candle-lanterns, and let it shine full on his face under the miserable cowl. The myriad criss-cross wrinkles were picked out in shadows: what Peter now saw was a death's-head. Confidence evaporated and again came that overpowering feeling of helpless defeat that he had the first time they met.

"It may seem a puny attack that can be beaten back by a mere boy," said the Ancient. "But if we take away the comforting ideas that keep men going, what have they left?"

Peter forced himself to speak. "Who are 'we'?"

The Ancient merely smiled. Again Peter had the feeling that there were more figures behind, watching in the shadows.

"Men will only have us left," continued the Ancient. "Once in history, now, we can appear as it suits us. And then we can retire to the background and watch things going inevitably our way."

"What way is that?" asked Peter.

"Watch carefully when you go back home," said the Ancient. "Look at the sorrow there will be in your own life. Look outwards and see the sorrow in the faces around you.

See the hate, see the anger. Watch the carelessness for life. And realize for ever that pleasure is only the respite of a moment from what we have designed for all time."

"If you are so powerful, why only deal with me and Gilbert and a few old plays?" asked Peter.

"We do it *because* we are so powerful," said the Ancient. "A single germ can start an epidemic. Despair has always been here: now we shall make it a galloping disease."

That was it. Despair. And despair was filling Peter from top to toe; settling on him just as the suffocating blanket had a few minutes before.

"My friends here will make it happen. Tell him, Cain."

One of the figures stepped forward.

"No crops, no food, no nothing," it said. Peter recognized it now as Cain, whom he had last seen running out of Goodybower.

"What have I left to live for?" Cain continued, in a curiously flat, monotonous voice, not at all like the ringing tones of the violent man in the acting area.

"Tell him, shepherds," said the Ancient.

Two more figures stepped forward.

"Bare soil; no sheep worth the name; those we have all skin and bone with no wool worth having," said one.

"Taxes to pay, mouths to feed, no hope," said the other.

Their voices too were toneless and dull.

"Tell him, Abraham," said the Ancient.

"God has no right to save my son," said the last figure. "I must kill him to keep him from the hopelessness that follows. And all must see me do it."

Then there was quiet. The candles flickered.

"I have my trusty servants here," said the Ancient. "Trusty servants who will go into the town with me and prepare for the day of the plays. And who will lock the door of this place behind them and place such a rock in front of it as will keep you safe here. And when your defeated friends think to look for you, time will have swallowed you up and you will be back in the hell of your own time, thinking of how you saw it all start. Goodbye, Master Peter."

And silently they left, Cain carrying one lantern, Abraham the other. Peter heard a lock turn and a heavy door swing on its hinges. He felt a draught of cold air from the open entrance. It crossed his mind to make a dash for it, but before he could move he heard a crash as the door was closed. Then a lock turned, and in a minute there was a reverberating bang as if a heavy weight had been pushed up against the door from outside.

Now it was pitch dark, very cold, and very, very smelly. And Peter was lonely. At least the Ancient had been company.

So that's it, thought Peter. There seemed nothing to do but to wait, to wait for the time of his entry back into the twentieth century. Gilbert, Giles, Francis and Gyll and their mother – none of them need ever have existed. All the strain, all the fear, all the hard work had gone for nothing. This was the end of his adventure. It had all been a complete waste of time.

The bubbling noises now sounded like laughter, directed at him. I'm nothing, thought Peter, but a great berk to be conned into all this.

Then Peter was aware of something that surprised him greatly. All this time, clutched in his hand, had been the little pipe that Francis had made for him. All of a sudden, he felt less alone. He sat down on the damp, dirty straw and started to play. The bubbling noises increased in number, as if in protest.

I know where I am, thought Peter. I'm in the dovecote.

Somehow this realization, and the possession of the little pipe, made him feel less totally miserable. To know where he was and to have something to pass the time with made his despair and loneliness more bearable.

So he settled down to wait, sometimes playing little snatches of tunes, sometimes dozing. And nothing happened.

– 9 –

GYLL

For a long time after everybody else had gone to sleep, Gyll lay awake. She was worried. She was ten years old; she had often been unhappy, often cold, often hungry. But she could not remember ever before being worried. Yet, if someone had asked her why she was worried, she would have found it very hard to give an answer.

She cast her mind back over the years. Ever since she could remember, the Corpus Christi plays had been the high-spot of her year – and everybody else's as well. The noise, the color, the life – they all mixed themselves up in her mind in a jumble of pleasure. And when the pleasure was over, she, her parents, everyone, would go back to work and resume their lives happy, certain once again that all was happening for the best no matter how hard things would seem when winter came again.

So why, this year, were things going wrong? Why were her father and Gilbert, the friend of all of them, going about with such grim faces, having long and muttered conversations so that nobody could hear them? What did all the odd things mean that had happened? – Cain knocking Abel out at the rehearsal, the three running men, the arrival of Peter.

Peter. His coming was the oddest thing of all. At first she had believed the story that he was a throw-out from a band of travelling actors. But why then couldn't he act? Perhaps that was why they threw him out. And what about his peculiar voice? And what about all the simple things he didn't seem to know? Francis was right; Peter really was the most ignorant person they had ever met. He knew nothing.

Then Gyll's mind uncovered for her what she had been trying all day to forget – the discovery she had made which alone was keeping her awake and which would never let her sleep.

Peter's shoes.

She had thought they looked strange the first night he had stayed with them. All through the afternoon of the next day – when they were rehearsing – she could not tear her eyes away from them. And when, late in the afternoon, Peter had taken them off – and his socks – to rest his feet, Gyll had picked each shoe up in turn when nobody was looking and looked at them carefully.

What she had seen had frightened her.

She did not mind that they were black and shiny. She supposed that a prince or a lord might have shoes of a leather as soft and smooth as this. She was mystified by the soles – made of a substance she had never seen before; hard and yet yielding, firm yet flexible. On these were strange designs – like the feet of animals. When she had gone outside she had seen, in the dust on the cobblestones, the same designs. Peter's shoes left a track. Was it a magic sign to ward off evil?

None of this could she understand. But equally none of it frightened her. It was when she thought of the stitching on the shoes that her stomach turned over. It was so neat, so hard to see; each individual stitch was so tiny. Gyll felt completely sure they could not have been made by any human hand. Only the Devil himself – she shuddered – could stitch leather like that.

But what was Peter doing wearing shoes stitched by the Devil? And if the Devil did the stitching, then what might be the animal tracks that the shoes left? Surely not . . . ? She liked Peter. There was nothing devilish, hellish, or evil about him. Gilbert liked him. Giles, her father, in spite of everything, liked him. Her mother thought the world of him. Francis could only be bothered to tease people he approved of – and anyway, he had made Peter a wooden pipe, a sure sign of friendship. Peter was the friend of all of them.

So why was he wearing shoes stitched by the Devil?

Many, many times did these thoughts wander round Gyll's head as she lay in her bed, listening to the soft snores of her parents. The night was still, soothing – but she was not tired. Once or twice she heard footsteps and voices in the street – but she took no notice. Then she heard a banging noise and more footsteps: she wondered what the disturbance was. It sounded like a downstairs shutter opening. Perhaps, she thought, Gilbert, Francis, or Peter wants some air.

Now the silence was again complete. Gyll thought it was taking whoever it was downstairs a long time to close the shutter. Her father would be very angry if he found a downstairs shutter was left open at night. She waited in suspense for the noise of its closing.

Gradually, the conviction that something was wrong stole over her. She got out of bed, threw a shawl over her nightdress, and tiptoed down the staircase into the lower room.

She gasped. It was as light as day. Moonlight flooded in through the completely-opened shutter. Gilbert and Francis slept on, as if the crack of doom itself would never wake them. But Peter's bed was empty.

She never quite understood why she did what she did next. She should have woken up everybody in the house. But she did not. She jumped lightly out of the window and ran quickly up the street toward Goodybower. Peter, she was sure, was up that way somewhere.

Out of the town she ran until she came to the acting area. It was completely quiet. The pageants stood silent in the moonlight. Hell mouth, indistinct, looked full of nameless menace. Wherever Peter was, he was not here.

So where could he be? Should she go home? She was just about to turn away when a thought struck her. Where she was standing was the very place that they had seen John Horne, Gibbon, and Parkyn running the way Cain had gone after the rehearsal. There must be a connection between them and Peter. So should she follow their route? But that would mean going into the Outwood, where it was dark, where spirits and demons lurked at night, hobgoblins and horrors too awful to be named. And who was to say she would find Peter at the end of it all?

She stood irresolutely. All sorts of reasons why she should go no further came to her. She was suddenly aware of cold, wet grass under her bare feet. She turned to go home – then, just as suddenly, wheeled round again impulsively and marched off into the darkness of the wood. There could now be no return.

The wood was full of noises: whirrings, clackings, screeches, whisperings, rustlings. Everything around her was alive. She was scared. What sort of life was it that she could hear? The Devil, she knew, could appear in many different guises. Trees stood out in stark relief as the moonlight filtered through gaps in their branches. Once an owl flapped past her. And she remembered the story told her by her father of the lay brother Adam who, with his servant, set out from his monastery to the nearby town on horseback. As they rode along, his horse's hair stood on end. For in front of them was a tree which seemed to be moving toward them. And though it was high summer, the tree was gaunt and covered in hoar-frost. They all knew it was the Devil. Adam, in spite of his horror and the fearful stench which came from the tree, exorcised it and bade the Devil leave it.

All for a while was well: but then the Devil appeared again, this time as a huge man. Adam hit out with his sword, but it was like hitting empty cloth. Then the Devil changed into a monk with a black habit and glittering, coppery eyes; then into an ass with huge ears. Adam and his servant drew a circle round themselves and made the sign of the cross – now the Devil could not come near them. But instead his ears changed to horns. Adam again hit out with his sword – but he hit the horns and it was like smiting marble. So the Devil changed into an owl and flew once round them; and then changed into a barrel and rolled away down the hill and into the town before them.

The story was true: Giles had said so, though it had happened a long way from Dunfield. And the proof was that for ever afterwards the poor horse was crazy.

Gyll tried hard not to think of such stories – but she took comfort from the fact that if Adam and his servant could survive such attacks from the Devil, then she could as well. Even so, she did not like to stop and look around her. The noises of the wood bore deep into her ears: the tiny cracklings, moanings, and rustlings nearly deafened her. A light wind rose; leaves and branches moved and waved before her eyes, and another story she had heard which concerned a man who had lived quite near Dunfield sprang unbidden into her mind.

He had been riding across a field full of growing rye which rippled in the wind. The rye parted – just as the leaves and branches of the trees seemed to be parting now in front of her – and a little man, entirely red, rose up from it. The little red man grew large until he seized the bridle and dragged both horse and rider away to a place where the rye seemed to grow high above all their heads. There they met a lady with her serving maids, and all were of great beauty. They pulled the man from his horse and tied him to the ground. The lady sawed through his head, took out his brains, and sealed his head up again. Then they let him go.

Crazed like a madman he went to a nearby town where a maiden took pity on him and tended his wounds. But for years the little red man haunted his dreams, until at last he went on pilgrimage to the shrine of St. John at Beverley. Here he fell into a deep sleep and dreamed a dream in which the lady appeared. She opened up his head and gave him back his brains: he woke up at last a happy and whole man.

So he married the maiden who had tended him and when she died he became a priest. One day when he was celebrating Mass the little red man came again to him and said, "Let the one you have in your hand guard you, for he keeps you better than I can."

The ending of the story cheered Gyll up a lot as she trudged on, especially as she had now come to the edge of the wood. In front of her were buildings – low down and some way to her left was the Manor House. It was dark: the Earl was away; only his bailiff would be there. It stood, dark and solid before her. A few score yards to her right was another bulky stone building – the dovecote. And as she looked she caught her breath in fear. For she was sure that, through the wooden vanes between the top of the wall and the roof itself, she could see flickering light.

Once again all her instincts told her to stay where she was: once again she jerked herself toward the dovecote, forcing her legs to move, one before the other, to within twenty yards of it.

Then, in front of her, she saw a bar of light – it started as a big vertical line, and grew wider until it was a square with a curved top. It was a door opening. Framed in the light from inside the dovecote were shapes of human figures. Out they walked – one, two, three, four, five. But they cast many little shadows in the artificial light from the door and huge, grotesque shadows on the stone dovecote wall in the moonlight and Gyll could not easily tell shadows from substance. Were there five men or six, seven, eight, nine? She could not say.

But she saw the light go out, heard a key turn in the lock and then realized three of the men were manhandling a huge block of stone up against the door so that, if it opened outwards (and she was sure it did), it would take a very long time to get it open even if the lock was picked.

Then the odd, black, frightening crew – five or nine or however many of them – shambled off into the blackness and were lost to sight in the wood.

As she watched them, all sorts of strange thoughts came into Gyll's mind. Who were they? What were they? She felt (though how could she be sure?) that one was Cain's build, and walked like him, too. The way the figure had helped shift the stone made her think of the way she had seen Cain stacking sheaves of corn.

And then a third story came into her head – why, she did not know – to make her shudder more than ever. A Friar who had once come to Dunfield to preach had told it in a sermon – and how well she remembered his screeching but riveting voice as the story shaped itself in her mind.

For there were three men of great riches in a certain town and they were supping ale in a tavern. And as the evening wore on, they fell to speaking of the life hereafter. And one said, "The priests deceive us who say our souls shall live on when our bodies die." And all laughed, until a man of giant stature whom they knew not came into the tavern and sat with them. "What do you talk of?" he said. "Why," said the man who had already spoken, "We talk of souls, how that they die with the body and need be taken no care of. Who wishes to buy mine may have it right cheap and we will drink away the profit together." Then said the giant, laughing, "Such a salesman as you have I long sought; name thy price." The man did so and at once the money changed hands. And for the rest of the evening the fellows drank on. But the time to leave drew near, and soon the giant cried, "Now must we go to our homes. But, before you leave me, tell me this. If a man buys a horse, and that horse still wears its reins, does not the man buy the reins as well?" And the companions all said, "Yes." So the giant at once seized the man who had sold his own soul and, before the very eyes of all present, vanished with him into thin air, with a roll of thunder and a flash of lightning. And only then did the companions realize that they had supped with the Devil but, in truth, had used no long spoon.

Gyll gained no comfort from this story at all – though perhaps she felt she had a glimmer of understanding of the behavior of Cain and the shepherds. But the longer she crouched in the grass near to the bulky dovecote and the more she thought about all she had just seen, the colder she became, and the more she shivered, in fear as well as in freezing.

What was she now to do? Her body seemed stuck to the ground, her mind capable of no more thought. Misery joined cold and fear; yet she did not even have the heart to cry.

For a few moments she stayed there, still as a stone, blankly listening to the noises of the night. Then she became aware of a new noise, not a natural one at all; a high-pitched, perky series of notes. Was it a bird – a thrush or a robin? Not in the small hours of the morning surely, thought Gyll. Then, with a flood of happy relief in her heart, she knew what it was; a tune played inexpertly on a wooden whistle. It must come from Peter and he must be inside the dovecote, she thought. Without even considering how pleased and relieved Peter might be to hear her friendly voice call to him through the walls of his prison, Gyll sprang up and, careless of who or what she might meet in the Outwood, ran back toward the town, never pausing for breath until she reached the door of her own house.

– 10 –

ESCAPE

Who are they? thought Peter, when the voices outside first came to his ears. He was feeling stiff, cramped, desperately uncomfortable. Far from growing used to the thin, sour smell of the dovecote he had come to hate it. He had taken to breathing through his mouth – and even then the thought that he was somehow swallowing the smell made him feel sick. He spent long periods holding his breath till he was dizzy. He had blown tunes on the pipe; had fiddled uselessly with the door, pushed it, punched it, and shouted at it: the great iron handle and hinges just stared impassively back at him. His bare feet, as he moved over the hard floor, hurt him. He had never felt so lonely, so powerless, so beaten in his life.

What his eyes made out of the inside of the dovecote didn't help at all: straw on the floor, a high roof, with moonlight coming from the join of ceiling to wall in a way he could not quite fathom, and the rows and rows of black holes in the walls from which came the placidly stupid sound of the pigeons' cooing.

It's a big, stinking prison, thought Peter. I give up.

It had taken him a long time to reach this point. The voices came just when he was at his very lowest. Who were they? he thought. And he answered himself; it's the Ancient and his mates come back to have a quick gloat.

But he listened again; he was sure one voice was a girl's – was it Gyll's? Yes, he was certain of it, though he could hear no words. And the deep, echoing rumble – Giles's voice, surely. Gilbert's voice then detached itself, and a sudden peal of laughter had to come from Francis.

Then came a loud hail through the door: it was Gilbert's voice.

"Art there, Peter?"

"Yes," he called back, half-crazy with relief.

"Then stay there, lad."

"Not much choice," shouted Peter, happy none the less. He got up, slipped the pipe into the pocket of the nightshirt and walked over to the door.

"We'll be a while yet finding a way out," replied Gilbert. "Save thy breath."

There was more muttering, then grunting and strain-ing noises as if they were all trying to move some heavy weight.

"Nay, we'll not shift it," came Giles's voice after some minutes of this.

"Tie a rope round it and pull," came the voice of Francis.

A little space of relative silence followed while Peter wondered what on earth they could be doing, then Gyll's voice rang out with cries of "Heave" at regular intervals, just as in a tug-of-war. But this, too, obviously did not work.

"Let it stay," came Gilbert's voice.

I reckon I'm here for good, thought Peter, depression returning.

There was another muttered conversation, then he heard Gilbert's voice again.

98

"Peter. Canst hear me, lad?"

"Yes," said Peter.

"There's a great stone wedged outside the door. We can't shift it. It beats me how any mortal man could have put it there. So you'll never be coming out through this door."

"All right then," said Peter, his voice full of the misery he felt. "I'd better say goodbye now."

"Nay, lad," said Giles. "There's another way. But the work will all be done by thee. Francis has gone back to town to bring the gear. And here's what's to be done."

As Giles explained what he had to do, Peter's heart sank.

"I'll never manage that," he groaned.

"You must or we're finished," said Giles. "I'll tell thee what's happening here from outside. Here comes Francis back: now remember, he's got another length of rope, a flying-belt for an angel, and a saw. So we're ready. What's to do first, then? What did I tell thee?"

"Climb up the wall," said Peter unhappily.

"Then get on with it," said Giles shortly. "The nesting-holes will make good footholds."

"But what if the pigeons fly at me and peck my eyes out or something?"

"Any bird with no more wit than to live here until it gets ate is not going to bother about thee clambering past," said Gilbert.

"I hope you're right," said Peter. Climbing was easy enough. The holes were firm: they made excellent hand- and footholds. Several times, though, there was a live stirring only a few inches from his face; each time Peter flinched. Once, when a pair of tiny, surprised, beady eyes popped out from a hole to look at him, he nearly dropped off the wall altogether. But he managed to keep going, in spite of the stirrings and in spite of the increased number of quite frenzied-sounding bubbling noises which, so close, were almost deafening. When he reached the top, Peter realized to his surprise that, in all the time he had spent in the dovecote, he had not seen a single pigeon outside its nest.

He also realized something else. As far as he could see, there had been no point in climbing up at all.

"I can't get out through these," he called down to Gilbert. For – and this explained how the moonlight had come through between wall and roof – in front of him was a series of thick wooden slats, running horizontally and jointed in to vertical posts, set at six-foot intervals in the top of the wall. A sort of huge, wooden, and fixed Venetian blind, Peter thought – and the space between the slats was wide enough for a pigeon, and for Peter's arm, but never in a million years wide enough for Peter himself.

"That's why we've brought the saw," called up Giles. "Canst see us through the slats of wood?"

"No," said Peter. "They're at the wrong angle."

"All right then. Put one of thy arms through. Just let it out straight. Now, Francis will throw the rope up. It will take a few times to reach thee. Don't try to catch it – just let it loop over thy arm: then hold it with the other hand."

"'Tis coming now," cried Francis.

Peter heard a rush of air: then a slapping sound as the rope hit the ground beneath.

"Try again," said Giles.

This time in passing, it hit his hand and he was surprised at how heavy it was.

After four more goes, Peter felt the rough weighty rope fall on to his outstretched forearm.

"Got it," he called.

He dug his bare, sore feet hard into the nesting-holes, leaned forward so that his stomach was pressed hard against the wall, gingerly removed his right hand from the vertical post he had been grasping, and – feeling surprisingly safe although hanging on thirty feet above a hard floor – pushed his right arm out into the open air and gripped the rope hard in his fingers.

"Now what?" he shouted.

"I'm tying the saw to the rope," answered Giles. "Pull the rope up. You'll soon find the saw come to hand."

"What's it for?" asked Peter.

"Eh, listen to that." Peter wondered how it was he thought he had actually missed the jeers of Francis. "Doesn't tha know what a saw's for?"

"Of course I know what a flaming, rotten saw's for," cried Peter, stung. "But I don't see how it's going to help me up here."

"Quiet, Francis," said Giles. "And thank thy stars you're not up there instead."

"I'd have been down since Candlemas," said Francis. And then, shouting to Peter: "Saw the slats out with it."

Peter pulled the rope up.

"I can only just get the saw through," he cried. "I'll never cut the wood with it."

"Then saw at an angle," answered Giles. "Try the top slat first: the rest will be easy. Don't fret about the damage; I'll see the bailiff after."

Laboriously, Peter pulled the clumsy-feeling saw flat between the top slats, untied it and looped the rope round the vertical post to his left. He tried to make the saw's teeth bite into the wood but the angle at which he was forced to hold it was so shallow that it was clear that he would have to saw through a far greater thickness of wood than if there were room to hold it properly. Still, Giles was right: the rest, by comparison, would be easy.

It was hard work. The saw at first kept slipping out: Peter could not establish a rhythm. As he had to press himself forward against the wall to stay up at all, he felt he could not put any strength into the strokes. However, as if in answer to his thoughts, he heard Giles call up from below.

"Don't strain at it. It will be done no quicker."

Peter relaxed. Even so, the sweat soon poured down his forehead and a dull ache spread through his right arm; he thought he would faint long before he had sawed even through the first slat.

However, by dint of taking frequent rests he managed to saw the first slat out. To see it disappear in front of him and to hear a bump as it hit the ground outside – and then, through the space now made, to be able actually to see Giles, Gilbert, Francis, and Gyll huddled in a little group seemingly many feet below him, looking upward, their faces clearly-etched but grey in the dawn light, cheered him up enormously and made him feel he was as good as out of his prison already. Able to use the saw properly now, he knocked out six more slats to have an opening about five feet wide and thirty inches high.

"What next?" he called down.

"Pull on the rope," said Gilbert. "There's a belt on its way up."

"What sort of belt?"

"What I showed thee," shouted Francis. "What God and the angels use to come down from heaven. I asked thee to have a go on it. More fool you that you didn't."

He's right, for once, thought Peter. Resigned to something uncomfortable and – he had a horrible feeling – dangerous, he pulled the rope up again. He could see now the bulky-looking object moving jerkily up the outside wall as he pulled. It stopped as it fetched up against the post to his left: he leaned over in that direction and carefully manoeuvred it through the slats. It was a broad leather belt with a big brass buckle. At the back of it was an iron bracket to which the rope was very firmly knotted.

102

"Put it on," called Giles.

This was difficult. Two hands were needed; but Peter felt he still wanted one hand free to hold on with. However, he tried again to cling on with his feet shoved in the nesting-holes and his body braced against the wall, leaning out of the gap he had made as far as he could. Slowly he felt some sort of confidence returning as he found he did not at once fall to the ground below; in fact, he began to feel quite safe. The belt was very big and it had to be done up to the last hole to feel at all firm.

"It's on," he called at last.

"Right. You must trust us," called Giles. "We will hold the rope taut. So climb out of the gap."

"How?" Now Peter was frightened.

"I care not how. Do it."

"I can't."

"You must. Or else stay here. We'll not let thee fall."

I'll have to trust them, thought Peter. But he looked down – and Giles, Gilbert, Francis, and Gyll seemed to be far away at the foot of a deep precipice.

Peter pondered. If I were at home I would think nothing of opening a window, putting my feet out, and sitting on the window-sill. So why not here? But I'll have to hold on very tight, and keep my head forward, because the gap is not very high and I could knock myself out if my head hit the edge of the roof. Anyway, I'll have to try it.

Very timidly he put both his hands on top of the wall and lifted first one leg, then the other over, until he was half sitting, half crouching inside the gap he had made with the saw, hanging on for dear life. He felt the belt pull in on his stomach as the rope behind him tautened as the others took the strain. Peter was, in effect, now hanging from the vertical post.

"Let go," called Giles.

"I can't," cried Peter.

And he couldn't. He daren't.

"Let go. Or we'll pull thee off. And that will hurt."

It needed a supreme effort to will himself into letting go. But he did; and when he did there was a glorious feeling of release. The rope ran smoothly round the vertical post, and Peter descended like a load on the end of a crane. He was gliding effortlessly through the air. Down he came, feeling the cool, fresh, early morning air caress his face, as the others carefully controlled the rope.

"Look at me. I'm flying," he couldn't help calling.

His feet gently touched the ground. "That was great," he said. "Pull me up again. Let's have another go."

"Don't talk daft," said Giles.

"We'd all like a go," said Gilbert. "But there's no time. It's sleep for thee. There's much to do."

"How did you know I was here?" said Peter.

"I found thee," said Gyll proudly.

"Later," said Gilbert. "Come home."

So, almost light-headed with relief and – he realized as soon as Gilbert reminded him of it – half-dead with fatigue, Peter walked back home with the rest of them through the Outwood.

He was happy. No matter what difficulties lay ahead – for he had gone miserably to bed, he recalled – he was glad to be back.

It was fast growing lighter. To the east the sky was touched with gold: when they emerged from the Outwood they felt in their bones that a day of glorious weather was coming. When they reached home Giles's wife was there: she gave Peter a mug of milk she had heated up for him and then pushed him into bed. But he needed no pushing: straight away he slipped into a deep sleep, as the sun climbed high in the sky outside and the little town began to move again.

– 11 –

DEVIL'S SHAPE

It was noon before Peter awoke, and once again it was a clear, hot day. The afternoon saw him rehearsing once more, with Giles – always hard, firm but fair – as demanding and impatient as he had been on the previous day. But there were big differences. This time, Peter felt he could take it; the strange experience of the night before – though still he didn't really understand it – had somehow hardened him and made him surer than ever that what he was doing mattered a lot. Also – to his surprise and very great relief – the rehearsals now seemed easy. The mess of words in his mind the day before had whirled round, settled down, and, while he was thinking about and doing quite other things, sorted themselves out.

Before they started rehearsing, Peter had told Gilbert and Giles everything that had happened the night before from the moment the shutter had been forced open. They had listened gravely and attentively. They made Peter repeat several times what he could remember of the words the Ancient had spoken.

"So he thinks thou'rt back in thy own time," said Gilbert when he had finished.

"Well, he's not," said Giles. "Yon old fellow's finished."

Gilbert didn't answer, but he frowned slightly, and Peter wondered what he was thinking.

"Get on with rehearsals," he said at last. "I'm off out."

And away he went. Giles and Peter – this time with Francis and Gyll – walked through the two plays time and again. Peter steadily grew in confidence, feeling he understood now more of the characters he was playing. The words of Cain, the shepherds and Abraham the night before in the dovecote had stayed in his mind. He felt the trust Isaac had in Abraham, the incredulous but unquestioning fear at being cast as the sacrifice, the glorious relief at realizing this was not to be. *For fear, sir, I was nearly mad,* said Isaac at the end. But if the Abraham of last night had his way, Peter would never have the chance to say those words himself. Daw, the third shepherd, took shape as a person with more in him than the other shepherds, just as Peter had thought on the first night. He was struggling for survival like the others – and also he was sharp, fair-minded, seeing more and further than his masters. After all, it was he who argued against hanging Mak and – remembering how Giles and Gilbert had argued about the play on the first day – Peter marked this as a point which might later prove important.

"Why, listen to him," cried Francis after they had been through the plays three times without a hitch. "He's a marvel."

Gyll smiled but said nothing. Peter guessed she was smiling for both of them – himself and Francis. There had been nothing forced in the praise Francis had given him.

"Aye, he'll do," said Giles, and went in the back room to join his wife.

Peter felt a great thrill of pride and relief. That offhand grunt from Giles was what he had been waiting for. Giles was satisfied – so he must be good. He was able at last to do what he had come for. He felt like jumping in the air and cheering.

"Come on, let's see what's doing up by Goodybower," said Francis, and the three of them raced out of the house and through the little streets brooded over by the tower of the great church. They didn't stop until they were sitting, breathless but happy, on the raked seating over the acting area, just where they had met each other for the first time two days before.

A marvellous sight met their eyes. The play of Noah was in rehearsal and Noah was building his ark. From what looked like a great heap of wood in the middle of the stage he selected first one piece and then another – and to Peter's amazement a real, big, and superb boat took shape. And Noah spoke as he built it.

> *Now my gown off I'll cast: I'll work in my coat.*
> *I must make the mast before I move one more foot.*
> *Ah! my back! It will burst. This is a sorry note.*
> *It's a wonder I last, such an old dote,*
> *All dulled,*
> *To begin such a work.*
> *My bones are so weak*
> *That no wonder they creak,*
> *For I am right old.*

"'Tis another of Gilbert's plays, this," said Francis.

"Look, there he is," said Gyll, pointing. Next to the Heaven Pageant sat Gilbert, his head in his hands, unmoving, looking as though he were in another world.

"We'll go and see him," said Francis, springing up.

"No," said Gyll quickly. "Leave him. He'll not want us. He wants quiet."

Peter knew Gyll was right, for it was obvious that Gilbert was deep in thought. But he said nothing, though the sight of Gilbert sitting there formed a little cloud in his new-found happiness.

Noah and his wife were fighting, because she would not board the ark, though Noah insisted disaster was imminent. Noah was little and old; his wife was beefy, strong, and twice his size. And she had a big voice too.

Noah shouted his puny loudest.

I'll strike you dead as a stone, you beginner of blunder.
I'll beat you, back and bone, and break you asunder.

They fought long and violently, rolling over and over the stage, pummelling, scratching, and kicking each other. Then came the wife's bellowing voice:

Out, alas! I am gone. Out upon thee, man's wonder. Noah replied, on his back on the stage, being sat on:

Hark how she groans, and me lying under.
But, wife,
I'll stop hitting you;
My back's broke in two.
Said the wife:
I'm all black and blue;
I'll never thrive.

The three children watched the play unfold, laughing as Noah and his wife scrambled up, dusted themselves down, and, shame-faced, boarded the ship; holding their breath as the Ark plunged into a flood made by a downpour lasting forty days (here squashed into three minutes). And at last, Noah, his wife, his sons and daughters-in-law all walked off the Ark in safety, peace, and unity, where only a little while before they had all been at each other's throats.

"Aye," said Gyll, sighing with satisfaction. "That's as it should be."

The actors and the Pageant Master had grouped in the middle of the arena, by the Ark, loudly discussing the rehearsal. Francis stood up.

"Ee, they'll be at that for hours," he said. "We'll have a look round. I'll show thee some more things as I've made."

Peter remembered how Francis had been talking, the day before at the midday meal, about the throne for Caiaphas. He asked if he could see it.

"Aye," said Francis, obviously pleased. "'Tis round here – we've been storing our gear in Hell for safe keeping."

So once more Peter found himself behind Hell mouth; a room now full of objects from the plays – but this time they entered it through a door in the back of the pageant.

"It makes a good store-room and saves a lot of carrying things around on the day itself," said Francis.

The throne was very big, carefully carved, and – though then it was still unfinished – intricately painted; and how proud of it Francis was. Peter was most admiring. All I can do, he thought, is to make plastic models of "Evening Star."

Gyll jumped up on the throne – when she stood on the seat, her head could not look over the top of the back.

"'Tis a right big chair, this," she said. "I'm shocked you had the patience, Francis."

"Well, I have," said Francis. "I took a long time over it, so just keep thyself away. Get off."

"I'll not," said Gyll, and, laughing, began to hoist herself with her arms over the back of it. The throne teetered backwards and was on the point of overbalancing, solid and heavy though it was.

"Get off," cried Francis in alarm, and he and Peter jumped forward to hold the throne down.

"That I'll not," cried Gyll.

Peter saw a look of anger coming over Francis's face, so he thought he had better change the subject for them. He didn't want to take sides, so he opened the nearest box to him and shouted, "Look at these," without even pausing to see what it was he had uncovered.

The box was full of devils' costumes. They were dark red, fitted with horns, leering and twisted masks for faces and long ropetails with sharp wooden points, like stings, fixed to the ends.

"They're great," cried Peter, and before the other two could say a word he pulled one on. It was too big, but when tied round him properly was quite comfortable, though heavy and hot. He felt a strange recklessness as soon as he was wearing it. Are these things all they're afraid of? he thought. The memories of the previous night seemed to grow dim.

"You put one on too," he said.

"Not us," said Francis.

Gyll was still standing on the throne. She looked at Peter as if horrified at what he was doing.

Peter delved into the box again.

"What's this," he said, as he pulled another object out.

It was a hunting horn. He tried to blow it, but could make no sound. It was obviously for the Devil in the Judgment Play – the one with the funny name Gilbert had mentioned in the train. Peter could not recall it.

"I'd take them off if I were thee," said Francis.

"Never," said Peter. "What a load of rubbish you do talk. They're only bits of costumes. They don't mean anything."

Once again he rummaged around the box. There were five more devils' outfits inside; nothing else.

"You're silly. These are like in a pantomime for little kids," he said. "There's nothing to them. They're well made, though. I like the tails."

Francis and Gyll were still silent, watching him.

"I'd have thought you'd have known more by now," said Francis.

"You're not really frightened of them, are you?" said Peter. "They're only cloth and old rope. These tails won't sting you or anything. I'll show you."

110

"Don't be daft. I know they'll not sting," said Francis. "But I don't like hearing thee laughing at them."

"Tell that to the man who painted the walls in the Chantry Chapel," said Peter. "You can see he laughed at devils."

"Aye. And he painted Hell mouth here, an' all," said Francis. "So think on that."

"There's nothing here to be afraid of," said Peter. "Look. I'll show you what I think of devils."

And with a length of twine he found on the floor, he took the tails of the five devils and tied them tightly just behind the wooden stings. Then he dragged the costumes behind him round and round the little room.

"I'm the King of the Devils," he chanted at the top of his voice as he marched along.

There was silence, so he continued.

"I'm leading all the revels," he yelled, feeling rather pleased with himself at making up such a good rhyme.

Still there was silence. So he stopped, now feeling a bit foolish, and looked at Francis and Gyll. But they were staring straight past him – toward the doorway. Slowly he turned – and there was Gilbert, standing there, transfixed, his mouth working soundlessly.

He's never afraid too? thought Peter. Then? – and the realization made him groan inwardly – he realized what Gilbert was seeing; a person in devil's shape, holding a horn, just as in the dream that had started his agony.

"It's all right. It's only me," said Peter, and struggled out of the costume before Gilbert could be any further alarmed. But this only seemed to make things worse. Gilbert struggled for words for a moment, then he burst out, "The tiger let inside the gates."

He's said that before, thought Peter. When?

"You should be home. You should be home," shouted Gilbert at Peter. "Dost think this business is over, then? 'Tis

Pageants of Despair

not, I'll tell thee; not by a long chalk. Dost think all they'll do is lock thee up in a dovecote? By God's bones they can do more, so think on. You should be home and not show thyself. I'll have words to say to that Giles, letting thee out. I come here to think on t' next move and here I find thee, and thou art *him* – him in my dream. Who art thou? What devil stood at my back and told me to bring thee? The tiger let inside the gates. You should be home."

And he turned on his heel and walked away.

Peter sheepishly took off the rest of the costume. He picked up all the devils' clothes and the hunting horn and shoved the lot back in the box.

There was a silence. Nobody seemed to have the heart to say anything. Then Gyll spoke.

"I'd like to ask who thou really art, but I mustn't, I suppose. You've never said what you were doing in t' dovecote."

"Don't ask him, Gyll," said Francis. "Me Dad says 'tis all right, so that's good enough. After Corpus Christi they'll tell us."

"I've upset him," said Peter, who was thinking only of Gilbert. "I didn't mean to. I should have known it was stupid, putting those things on."

He knew he had been foolish, and yet didn't quite know what had come over him. The suspicion was in his mind that he might have done more to Gilbert than just upsetting him.

"Hast got thy pipe, Peter?" said Francis. "We'll give ourselves a tune on the way home."

In his pocket Peter found the pipe Francis had made for him. It was odd, he thought. He had not yet possessed the pipe for twenty-four hours, yet already he did not like to be without it. The two of them managed a reasonably perky little march to walk home to, while Gyll sang and whistled in accompaniment. But they knew, as they walked along in the late afternoon sunshine, that the carefree feeling of an hour or so before had gone. Whatever they felt, it was not what had made Gyll so happy at the end of the Noah play.

— 12 —

THOUGHTS IN SOLITUDE

Supper was gloomy; so was the rest of the evening. Gilbert had returned an hour after the children and, having eaten his supper, had stalked straight into the back room, motioning Giles to join him. Giles's wife came scurrying out and she and the children sat miserably while Giles and Gilbert raged at each other behind the closed door. Not many words could be made out, but the bones of the argument were clear enough. Giles thought that all danger had passed and that Peter could do what he liked until the day of the plays. Gilbert thought that danger was still very close to them and that Peter must remain a virtual prisoner. This would have been no more than a difference of opinion had not Giles already let Peter out – it was this, coupled with the severe fright Peter had given him at the Hell Pageant, which made Gilbert so furious. If Gilbert was in fact suspicious of Peter because he had appeared dressed as the Devil with the Horn, he did not say so – though throughout supper he had looked strangely at him.

One speech of Gilbert's had sounded out clearly.

"He's been running round town all day so that anyone could have seen him; if *they've* seen him, we might as well have got ourselves a good night's rest last night, instead of making shift to get him out of t'dovecote."

Giles's reply was inaudible, but it seemed to Peter there were two things he could have said; either that the Ancient and his men had shot their bolts and last night had seen the last of them, or that they had spotted Peter that day – in which case he might as well now go wherever he wanted, for one may as well be hung for a sheep as a lamb. There was a third possibility – that he had not been seen; that as far as the Ancient was concerned Peter was away back in his own time, leaving the dovecote to the smell and the pigeons. In that case he would have to stay hidden.

It was this last possibility that Gilbert believed. The door of the back room opened and he came through it, shouting over his shoulder at Giles, "He'll stay in this house and he'll not leave it till it's time for him to get on t' stage."

With that he marched through the front room and outside into the street. They didn't see him again that evening.

Giles followed him through the door and slumped into a chair.

"He's off to get drunk," he said. "He's fair wild about it all."

He looked gloomily at the floor for a while. Nobody spoke.

"I reckon he's right," said Giles at last. "But it will mean tha'll not see t'procession tomorrow – at least, not close to. Happen you'll see some of it through t' window. Anyway, you can go through t'lines in t'play to pass time away."

What a terrible prospect, thought Peter, very disappointed. However, he was here to do a job, he supposed, so he thought he had better make the best of it.

The evening wore on. Francis and Gyll did their best to raise everybody's spirits; their mother helped – but it seemed nothing could shake off Giles's depression and Peter, still upset by the afternoon's episode, kept wondering what was likely to happen to Gilbert. When it was dusk, Giles, who had been fidgeting impatiently for some time, said, "I can't stop here: I've work to do," abruptly stood up and walked outside, slamming the door behind him. And, like Gilbert, he was not seen again before they all went to bed.

For the first time, Peter had an uninterrupted night's sleep. And how he needed it – he woke up the next morning totally refreshed. He was roused early, for all the others were up to prepare for the procession. Giles and Gilbert had returned and were up with the rest of them, though Gilbert was very bleary-eyed and bad-tempered, complaining all the time of a headache and a wish to eat no breakfast.

"Tha shouldst drink less and think more," said Giles. "I've no sympathy with thee – I've been working all night."

"Anyway, what's going to happen?" asked Peter quietly of Gilbert.

Gilbert's eyes seemed to focus on him with difficulty. "Eh? – oh, aye, well – 'tis what I were telling thee on the walk here three days ago," he said. "There's a service and then the Pageants are pulled all round t'town boundaries and then down to Goodybower, where we leave them for t'night."

He no longer seemed to have the air of suspicion with which he had treated Peter ever since the incident with the devil's costume. He seemed somehow resigned to failure. He looked haggard, more dark-jowled than ever; as if the waiting for the next day were proving too much for him.

"Giles has been up all night seeing his Pageants are ready and in t' right places," he went on. "I should have helped, I suppose. Still, there'd be enough there and glad to do it – I wouldn't be missed."

"Well," said Peter, feeling rather at a loss for words as this cowed manner in Gilbert was new to him, "I hope you have a good time."

It was an inadequate thing to say and it sounded odd as he said it. But he could think of nothing else – especially as he was still feeling left out and envious of the others.

"By God's bones, I can't see that happening," said Gilbert. "I'm sorry for thee, though, having to stay here. But 'tis best, lad, 'tis best. I'm sure of that."

In his heart, Peter was sure of it too – and that made their leaving him more bearable. Otherwise, the sheer excitement of Francis and Gyll, which he could not help but notice although they tried to hide it from him, would have upset him too much.

"I wish tha wert with us today," said Gyll just before they left. "But tha'll still be here when we come back, and we'll tell thee all there is to know."

So out they all clattered and the little house seemed very quiet when they were gone. He watched after them through the window: he could see their path right up to the great church. The bells were ringing: people were beginning to converge from all directions. In front of the church stood the Pageants: colorful, flag-bedecked, ready for performance but as yet deserted.

Giles walked on, his wife leaning on his arm. Francis and Gyll ran on before in short bursts and then stopped for the others to catch up. Gilbert followed, stalking alone behind the rest. Then they were swallowed up in the great press of people making for the church.

Soon, nobody was to be seen at all – everybody was in the church. The sun rose higher: an hour passed. Then out of the church they swarmed in their hundreds: priests, musicians, actors, and people. Now the Pageants were occupied: horses were attached to the shafts: the procession formed. A great Cross was raised and the whole colorful, noisy, long phalanx moved off and out of Peter's view.

Then there was silence. He was completely alone – probably the only person left within the boundaries of the town.

The day dragged for Peter. He spent a little time going through his parts in the plays. He arranged the room to look like the acting arena, constructing his own Hell and Heaven out of chairs and the table and then, on his own, dashed around performing all his moves to his shadow and shouting his words to thin air. Not for the first time he wished he had been able to go through the plays with the actors he would meet on the day – but that, he supposed, would have been impossible. It would have helped him a lot to get used to the acting arena at Goodybower – but that would have been difficult too if his mission was to be kept secret. He fell to thinking of the day of the plays itself – and then realized, with a sudden shaft of fear, that it was *tomorrow*. The very next day he would be doing all this – for real! The knowledge had been dimly in his mind all the time, of course. Now it had pushed itself to the front, and he had to sit down to get used to it.

He was fairly sure now that he could do the acting: he could make some sort of fist at it at least. He was able, he thought, to keep his eyes open, to spot anything unexpected, to be able to deal with any strange things that might happen on the stage. He had seen the men in the dovecote, and so he thought he knew where the danger would come from, though he did not know what danger it would be.

And after his night in the dovecote he had a slightly clearer idea of what it was all about.

For the first time he began seriously to think of the words the Ancient had used. "Sorrow," he had said. "Despair," he had said.

Then the full words of the Ancient came into his mind, and for a moment he was back in the cold, smelly dark, with the decrepit face framed by candles hovering in the air before him.

"Watch carefully when you go back home. Look at the sorrow there will be in your own life. Look outwards and see the sorrow in the faces round you. See the hate. See the anger. Watch the carelessness for life. And realize for ever that pleasure is only the respite of a moment from what we have designed for all time."

That distant voice seemed to sound from inside his own head – and it made him recall things that Gilbert had said to him. But what did it all mean? Then, as if for the first time for days, Peter recalled his real situation. He was on a journey, from London to Dunfield. He had not yet arrived. He did not know when he would arrive, nor what he would find when he did. And still he did not know what he had left behind him. Yes, there was a sorrow in his life. But how big was it? Would it pass? Would his mother return, her old self again? Did it depend on him what would happen? Was it that the triumph of the Ancient would mean, for Peter, the greatest sorrow? That last night at home had never been far from his mind. But now it came back with such vividness that he almost relived it, and with the mental picture came an impatient wish for the plays to be started, so that he could be doing something himself to defeat the Ancient. He found himself fidgeting; almost bursting with impatience. Why couldn't the next day be here already?

Sometimes he could hear cheering and shouting as from some way off as the day wore on. Now, however, he did not feel at all envious of Francis and Gyll in the procession; he just wished it was all over. Out in the scullery he found some scraps of meat, some bread, and some milk – these kept hunger away. But he had no real appetite. For once the tunes he played on the wooden pipe gave no solace. He just wanted to be getting on with what he had come to do.

The day wore on; the sun began to sink. The streets filled up with people, laughing, shouting, drinking, fighting. Giles and his family and Gilbert came home, ate, and drank. Once again Giles and Gilbert went out, this time to make all ready for the next day's plays. The curfew rang out from the tower of the church. And Peter was feeling so keyed up that he could pay no attention to anything. All that the others told him – of the procession, the progress of the pageants, the crowds of people, the joy, the life, the activity – mattered nothing to him.

When night and sleep came, Peter could think only of one thing. It's tomorrow. Tomorrow is the day it all happens. I will make it happen.

And he slept like a log till sunrise.

– 13 –

CAIN AND ABEL

Sunrise came, the whole town awoke. In what seemed an incredibly short space of time, Peter found himself out of bed, out of the house, at Goodybower, and – dressed in a short, white tunic – sitting on the stage of the Abraham and Isaac Pageant, waiting for the performance to start.

Once again, the morning was blue and clear; the rising sun was quickly growing hotter. Shadows were still long, though, and Peter sometimes shivered slightly in the thin tunic. Goodybower was alive with people. The pageants for the Cain and Abel, Noah, and Abraham plays were already in place, in gaps between the seats. Behind them stood more pageants for more plays, waiting to be moved up when the plays before were finished. All were brightly painted – reds, greens, yellows, blues, and golds stared out in the sunlight. They were decked with flowers, flags, and bunting. More flags waved over the banks of seats, which were filling up quickly. The mayor, corporation, and burgesses of the town entered, many in gorgeous but surely too hot blue and red fur-lined robes; also entered the main tradesmen and masters of the Gilds. They took the best seats: boxes at the top.

Below them swarmed in a noisy, fighting, pushing mass; the rest of the people – hundreds upon hundreds of them, or so it seemed; a good-humored crowd, shouting, laughing, and happy.

Soon the arena was full; the awkward, spidery, wooden skeletons of seats were smothered in rows of packed bodies. Once again, just as on the day of his arrival, Peter was reminded of a football crowd. There was the same atmosphere of riotous expectancy – an atmosphere which infected Peter so that he almost forgot the sinking fear he felt about his own appearance – now very near – in front of them.

Francis and Gyll had disappeared early on. Giles and Gilbert stood with Peter, one on either side – he thought he knew what a boxer must feel like with his seconds giving last-minute advice. He kept his eyes looking forward, out at the rowdy bright exterior. But he was conscious of the cool, quiet, dark dressing-room at the back of the Pageant that he had just left. Noise and color in front; shady silence behind – but in spite of all the sound outside, the three of them became aware of the padding of footsteps on wood behind them. Someone else was coming out of the dressing-room into the sunlight.

They turned. It was a man, probably in his forties, balding and greying. His face was thin, his eyes were dark. He slouched across the pageant stage.

"'Tis a bright day, Parkyn," said Gilbert.

The man only grunted. But the grunt was enough for Peter to be sure – this was Abraham. First the slouch had seemed familiar, then the grunt, little though it was, had reminded him straight away of the dead, dragging voice in the dovecote – "I must kill my son."

He shivered again.

But Abraham showed no interest in him – or in anyone else. Something about him indefinably reminded Peter of

122

a clockwork motor that had run down and was waiting for someone to wind it up again. He sat down on the edge of the pageant stage and never moved again until his play started.

There was little time for worry about Abraham, however. Someone else came bounding out of the dressing-room.

"Wheer's me smock? I can't find t'clothes as I've got to wear."

It was a boy of about Peter's age – and he was very angry.

"Giles – tha never forgot to tell t'lad he'd not be doing t'part?" said Gilbert.

"By God, I did," said Giles, and hastily took the boy on one side. What he said Peter could not make out; but he heard the chink of money and saw the boy's anger die very quickly.

"Next year, lad," said Giles, as he moved back to them. "I promise thee."

"Right-oh, Master Giles," said the boy as he ran off into the crowd. "I'll keep thee to it."

I wonder, thought Peter.

"Hast tha sorted it out wi't'lad in t'Shepherds' Play?" said Gilbert.

"I'd best make sure," said Giles. "But later; there's near all day for that."

Peter was surprised that a man who wanted everything just so in the acting of the plays should have forgotten something as important as that. He knew that if he had been deprived of his big moment in the same way, he would have been furious.

But Gilbert was not surprised at all.

"That's the trouble with thee, Giles Doleffe. Thou'rt too busy thinking as thou mak'st things work all by thyself; don't forget the people as makes them work for thee."

"Shut thy row," said Giles, disgruntled.

"Tha'd do best as a puppet-maker, not working with real people," said Gilbert. "Get thyself off and look for t'boy."

"Later," said Giles.

And Peter couldn't blame Giles for not wanting to go then. For the plays were starting. First came the musicians – a parade of them walking across the arena to take up places by the Heaven Pageant. They carried and played a motley collection of instruments – harps, handbells, drums, a long, straight trumpet, and flutey-sounding instruments which seemed to Peter like the recorders he once played at school. The noise of the band was tuneful, rhythmic – yet, to his ear, slightly odd.

Then, opposite them, on the Heaven Pageant, appeared God – a majestic figure in white and gold – flanked on both sides by his angels. In a ringing voice which seemed to fill without effort the whole of the packed bowl of quiet, intently listening people, God told how he would create the earth. Simple verse with a measured rhythm.

There followed the battle in Heaven between the good and evil angels; the fall of Lucifer; the raising up of Adam and Eve – then Lucifer spoke his warning to mankind:

Now man is in Paradise:
But he shall go, if we be wise.

After the tempting of Eve it was the end of the first play. Hell mouth opened; Lucifer and the fallen angels disappeared into it; it closed. The upper ridge of teeth fell solidly and the two rows ground together. The complete attention of the audience lifted a little – there was a collective sigh over the whole of the arena. The tension broke; first one excited conversation started, then another, until, within seconds, there was a noisy babble of voices. Nobody paid any attention to the fact that the Cain and Abel Pageant was in position and that from it a small figure was trying to make himself heard. It was Cain's servant, waving his arms and yelling at the top of his voice.

"Keep going, lad," said Gilbert.

Fellows, shrieked the servant. *I forbid*
Any other noise or cry.
The man who dares do such a deed –
The devil hang him up to dry.

He began to get through to the audience; they ceased their noise and turned their attention to the play – which, after all, was a new one to them.

Both Giles and Gilbert stiffened: Peter caught the tension in them and shared it himself. Now would be the first inkling of how the day would go.

"Be ready," said Gilbert. "We'll not be afraid to dash on if we're wanted."

"Abel will keep out of trouble," said Giles – though he sounded far from convinced.

"He'll not know where trouble's coming from," said Gilbert.

Cain and the servant were arguing over the plough – a real one drawn by oxen and horses – and Cain was indeed a fearsome sight. Once again, Peter sensed the power that seemed to radiate from him; he dominated his servant – and the audience. And Peter remembered those two long and strong arms that had dragged him out of the house and bundled him off to the dovecote.

When Abel appeared, he seemed puny and insignificant by comparison.

"He could crack him like an eggshell," groaned Gilbert.

What was going to happen, then? Peter asked himself. Just a repetition of the rehearsal, but this time with the real death of Abel?

"He could kill him and then laugh at us," went on Gilbert.

Giles was silent.

"And then we're finished. Before Peter even goes on. For everything else will be moonshine," said Gilbert.

"T'lad out there's not daft," said Giles.

"But he's little," said Gilbert.

"Watch," said Giles.

"'Twill be no fair fight," said Gilbert.

The watching crowd seemed to seize this feeling; a sort of muttered gasp of sympathy sounded from all around – as if here was a David and Goliath contest which everybody knew in advance would end in the wrong way. Everybody's sympathies were with the soon-to-be-murdered Abel, whose firm, young voice was now heard.

Come forth, brother; let us go
To worship God. We are so slow.
Let us give him part of our fee;
Corn, cattle, whatever it be.

The crowd were with Abel. Peter could feel the sheer force of the attention they were paying. Nearby were people with brown, dirty, knobbly faces whose lips were working as if they were speaking Abel's lines with him. At the same time could be heard from others a low whispered, "Aye."

Abel finished speaking. There was a moment's silence. Then Cain wheeled round on Abel, and the violence of his movement caused an involuntary gasp from the crowd. His voice, harsh, vibrant, carrying to every corner, rang out.

What? Let out your geese; the fox will preach.

That was to the audience. To Abel he said:

How long will you try to teach
Me with your sermonizing?

There was real anger in his words, as of a man who is tried to the uttermost. He went on,

Shall I leave my plough and everything,
And go with you to make an offering?

126

Nay, thou'lt find me not so mad.
Go to the devil, and tell him I bade.
What gives God thee to love him so?
He gives me naught but sorrow and woe.

"And me," came an unexpected voice from somewhere in the crowd over to Peter's left. Heads turned to where the interruption had come from; there was some disturbance and cries of, "Quiet!"

"Listen to Cain, I say. He's right," came the voice again.

Peter looked at Gilbert. "Is Cain right?" he said.

"Wait and see," Gilbert replied.

Cain and Abel were now arguing over the offering they were to give. But Cain turned away from Abel and began to speak to the audience – or, more particularly, to where the interruption had been.

When other men's corn grew fair and tall,
My crop never grew at all.
When I should have sown, and I wanted seed,
And of good corn had great need,
That God gave me none of his,
So none will I give him of this.
Don't be thinking I'm to blame,
If I should serve him back the same.

Cain was completely ignoring Abel. He had turned to the audience, and it was as if, while he was speaking, he was listening carefully to them, waiting for an answer of some sort. It came almost at once. For a muttering, most of it angry, built up. From the back came the same voice as before. "That's right, Cain, and 'tis the same for all of us. Why should we give up our goods to any God or Lord?"

"Aye," came a voice from the other side of the arena, "'tis all we ever get. Give God not a thing, Cain."

For a moment, there seemed chaos in the audience; confused voices struggling for expression.

"What's happening?" asked Peter.

"I do not know," said Gilbert. "Things are bad, as I had feared. But differently so."

"What shall you do?"

"What can I do? Even as I look, the day becomes too much to handle."

It looked as though he was right. Somehow the audience was out of control. It was true the play had gone on; Abel had been shouting his heart out, but not a word could be heard and, in truth, nobody was listening.

But then Cain drew breath and opened his mouth to speak – and at once there was silence. Everybody was rapt. And Peter knew now that it was Cain who had the control over them; like a great orator in a packed hall, he was holding them spellbound – and it seemed as if he was speaking to each person there individually.

The devil take me, I say, if
For as many years as I may live,
I give away my goods or gifts –
Any riches I might have won –
Either to God or yet to man.
For if I give away my goods,
Then I would walk with a tattered hood.
'Tis better to hold that which I have
Than creep from door to door and crave.

As the speech progressed, Cain's voice rose. Every word bit home to his audience. He was not acting; he was making a speech from the heart. He was not an actor impersonating Cain; he was Cain himself. And when the speech was finished, Peter was shocked by what followed. The audience gave a great cheer, a deafening roar, in which were let loose years of pent-up frustrations, and living with hunger, death – and delight at someone at last understanding.

128

"But they are *my* words," shouted Gilbert, trying to make himself heard. "They are my words he is using. Don't they understand? This is not what my words are for. He is using them for himself. But that is not what they mean."

"But Cain's right," shouted Peter. "It's not fair that he should give all his crops away to God. And it's not fair that the people have to give them all to the Lord of the Manor."

"I know, I know, I know," roared Gilbert. "I feel with these people more than they know; more than Cain and whoever is behind him. I want their good; he wants their damnation."

He moved to the edge of the pageant as if he were going to jump into the arena and argue with Cain himself. Peter and Giles darted after him and with difficulty pulled him back.

"'Tis no good," Giles shouted. "No one will hear thee. Let it die down."

Gilbert let himself be pulled back. Meanwhile, the play had gone on; Abel – though nobody could have heard him – had made his sacrifice. Cain's turn came. A little pile of sheaves lay on the ground; he started to count them out. But he was keeping the best for himself and giving for sacrifice the very thinnest and poorest. And each time he kept one for himself, the audience gave a little cheer. Peter was reminded of a film he had once seen of a bullfight and the cries of "Olé" from the crowd every time the matador made a pass at the bull. He realized even more how Cain had mastery of his audience. At least he thought, they are listening now. They even listened to Abel.

Cain, I beg – your sheaves so tend
That God in Heaven will be your friend.

There was at once a great roar of mocking laughter, and when Cain turned on Abel with his harsh, jeering voice,

Peter knew that the crowd's scorn was, like Cain's, all directed on to the puny figure of Abel.

How quickly they change, he thought.

Cain spoke.

My friend? He'd not be if he could.
I've never done him any good.
I tell you straight, he'll get no more.

Peter was just thinking how different was this subtle, calculating actor, able to play on the heartstrings of the audience, from the ranting maniac he had seen at the first rehearsal, when something else happened. When Cain tried to light his sacrifice, no flame appeared – just a thick cloud of grey, choking smoke, unlike the clear flame from Abel's. And when Cain rose, coughing and spluttering, and shouted again at Abel, a new voice was heard, this time from the Heaven Pageant. The magnificent white and gold figure of God appeared again, and delivered the speech Peter had heard on his first day in Dunfield.

Cain, why art thou such a rebel
Against thy brother Abel?
To jeer him when there is no need.
If thou tithe right, thou'lt get thy meed,
But be thou sure, if thou tithest ill,
I shall repay thy great evil.

Peter thought back to how horrified Francis and Gyll had been at Cain's answer to this, at that first rehearsal. Now the audience will come back, he thought. Certainly there was silence in the audience as they waited for Cain to speak – as if they felt that this time he had bitten off more than he could chew. How could he answer God back?

They soon found out – and Peter realized how changed things were: Cain's voice was a sneer, not a shout. It showed how confident he was.

Hey, who's that hob-over-the-wall?

130

Who was that who piped so small?
Abel, we'll leave these perils all,
God is out of his wits.

This last line made the audience nearly hysterical with laughter; for a full minute, roars and screams of glee rolled round the acting arena. And Gilbert sat powerless.

"They've gone mad," was all he could say.

But the laughter died as Cain spoke to Abel.

Hark; speak with me before you go.

Abel tried to move past him, but Cain blocked his way. His voice was now quiet; it was under control, but the anger underneath could be felt.

What? You thought you could escape me so?

And now there was a complete, absorbed silence everywhere. Nobody moved; nobody scraped a foot against a seat or shuffled on the benches for greater comfort. The crisis was here; so complete was the attention on the two figures in the center of the arena that Peter half expected them to catch fire and shrivel up under the sheer force of it.

Cain spoke once again.

You thief, brother. Why burned your sheaves so clear?
My sheaves only smoked
As if they'd have me choked.

And Abel answered, firm and clear,

God's will, I trust it were,
That mine burned so clear.
If yours smoked, am I to blame?

The tension was suddenly broken: a voice cried, "Kill him, Cain. He's a cheeky devil."

The cry was taken up all round. "Kill him, Cain. Kill him, Cain."

And so when the shouting died down and Cain picked up the jaw-bone lying on the floor, it really seemed that he was not doing things laid down for him in a script but acting on the advice of the audience.

Peter thought back to the first day, when he had seen Cain stand over Abel at the rehearsal in just the same way. The words were the same. The actors were the same. But all seemed utterly changed. Abel stood before Cain: the jawbone Cain wielded came toward him in a looping arc. Abel's hands, one clenched, came up toward his face as if in a vain attempt to ward the jaw-bone off: his face turned away from it. In the otherwise complete silence there sounded a click; a tiny little noise, which yet travelled to the ears of everybody present. Peter shuddered to think what it might be. He remembered the fresh-faced young man with the livid scar over one eye who had pleaded with Giles to stay in the play.

"I know my own brother; none knows him better," he had said. "He's big, but he's gentle. He'll not hurt me." How wrong can you be? thought Peter.

Almost as in a slow-motion film, Abel seemed to crumple. His face and arms had turned away from Cain and now he had his back to Peter. Awkwardly he hit the floor of the stage and lay there, dead still, on his face. To Peter's horror, blood started to flow from under his body and a relentlessly widening puddle formed all round him; it spread, except where it poured instead through cracks between the planks, until there was a crazily-shaped blot of congealing red surrounding the inert, sprawling figure.

Cain stood exulting over the body. To the audience he shouted again,

And if any of you think I did amiss,
If he comes up here I'll do worse than this
So that all men may see.
Much worse than it is
Right so it shall be.

When Peter had heard Cain say these words before, he had been defiant: now he was confident: he knew nobody would challenge him. He was right. Cries of encouragement came from the people; "Well done, Cain!," "Long live Cain!," and the like. And the cries swelled and broadened into a cheer which roared and redoubled as Cain turned and walked up to the Hell Pageant. In front of it he made a slight bow as if to somebody no one else could see and then – just as he had done before – walked past the Hell Pageant and over the quarry wall, where he stopped, turned, and saluted the audience with a wave of his hand. Then he ran away to be lost to sight once again in the trees.

Every eye was on him as he went; as he disappeared, the cheering died; soon, once again, there was silence. And while there was silence, Peter, Gilbert, and Giles ran out into the arena to the body of Abel. Gilbert turned him over and cradled his head as, with his cloak, he tried to wipe away the sticky blood in his hair and smothering his face.

"We should not have let thee do it. We should not have let thee do it," he moaned.

But if you hadn't, it might have been me there, thought Peter, with fear snatching at his heart.

Now Cain had disappeared, the crowd turned back to the stage. Suddenly a hot wave of anger and resentment from them seemed to flow down and envelop Peter, Giles, and Gilbert.

Gilbert felt it too, and said, "We must get out or they'll kill us."

For the crowd was roused: already some men were standing as if to march on to the stage. Gilbert stopped wiping Abel's face; instead he started to mutter and to cross himself – as did Giles. As for Peter, part of him felt such a sensation of hopeless fear as to make him shiver with cold on this hot day, while another part of him seemed to be detached, watching a drama which was happening to someone else.

Men now started to run toward them – and they must have been coming quite quickly, with murder in their hearts, but to Peter they seemed hardly to move.

Then something happened which caused all the men to stop in their tracks, and run back moaning; which caused women to scream and faint; which caused Gilbert to fall over backwards and rise to his feet, his face chalk-white; which made Peter wonder whatever sort of crazy dream he was having. It happened suddenly, with no warning. It changed everything.

Abel sat up.

"Eh, lads," he said. "I reckon I made thee fret a bit there."

"By God's sides," said Gilbert. "'Tis a miracle."

"Aye, Master Gilbert," said Abel. "I reckon thi play's over now: us can't keep going when t'main actor's gone running off. Come with me away from t' stage and I'll tell thee how to do a miracle."

So they walked off the stage, watched by a silent stupefied audience. And back in the pageant, while the others looked carefully at him as if they still could not believe their eyes, Abel spoke.

"I knew I'd have to be canny-like," he said. "So I thought out how to make him think he'd thumped me one. See here."

He opened his still-clenched hand. In his palm were two large pebbles. And he made the noise again: that clear click which had made Peter shudder.

"That to make thee think he'd fetched me one. And this to make thee think he'd done t'job proper-like."

And from inside his blood-soaked tunic, he produced a revolting (to Peter) looking red scrap of skin.

"We killed us pig this morning," he said. "We'll have leg of pork soon. And I cut out its bladder and filled it wi's blood. Then I stuffed it down t'front of my shirt. So when I fell over, I burst it, see? And I bet it gave thee all a good fright."

There was silence. Gilbert broke it.

"Tha've done wonders, lad. More than you'll know."

"What about me brother, then?" said Abel.

"Wait till nightfall," said Gilbert. "And he'll be back somehow. It depends on the day whether thou'lt want him back."

"Master Gilbert, stop talking in riddles," said Abel.

"'Tis only way I know, lad," said Gilbert.

"Peter," said Giles. "Tha'd best be on thy pageant now. Thou'rt Isaac in a minute."

Good Heavens, I'd quite forgotten, thought Peter. Somehow the events of the last few minutes had seemed the end of everything. But the crowd was quiet now: peace was restored – the plays had to continue and the play of Noah had started.

"'Tis up to thee, lad," said Giles as they walked behind the seats to the Abraham Pageant.

But whatever can follow Abel's performance? thought Peter. How can I match that?

They went in through the back of the pageant. Giles checked the props – the sword for Abraham and the sheep for sacrifice – and saw that the other actors – the servants – were in place. A waving hand from the Heaven Pageant told him God and the angel were ready.

"'Tis due to start," said Giles.

The Noah play actors were trooping off, pulling the ark behind them. An excited babble of talk broke out all over the arena: the crowd seemed to have forgotten the earlier shocks and now seemed relaxed and happy.

The band struck up. The figure of Abraham, who had been quite still all this time, seemed to come to life. Taking no notice of anybody else at all, he slowly rose and moved to the center of the acting arena; stiff, like a wooden puppet.

What's going on in his mind? thought Peter.

The music stopped. The play started.

Abraham's voice called out his sorrow and despair to God: God told him that, as a token of faith, he must kill Isaac.

Abraham's voice sounded out clearly: *Isaac, son, where art thou?*

And at that point, Peter, his heart beating wildly, walked out into the middle, feeling the hot sun on his head and hearing the curious whispering of the rows and rows of people seated all round him.

— 14 —

ISAAC

Many thoughts swirled round Peter's head as he moved out
into the middle. Chief among them was that he just didn't
know what to do. He knew the part now inside-out – but that
wasn't enough. Abel had thought it all out before; with proper
rehearsal and knowing what might happen, he had had a
chance to think out how to deal with the danger on the stage.
Peter had no idea at all except that he must not be where
he was supposed to be when the time for sacrifice arrived.

His first appearance was a short one.

I'm all ready, father. See me here –
Now I was coming to you.
I love you deeply, father dear.

Abraham looked hard at him; unblinking, intense eyes
that seemed to bore into his skull. When he spoke, Peter was
shaken to hear the heavy sarcasm in his voice. Abraham
surely doesn't talk like that, he thought.

Do you so? I would like to know
If you love me as much as you have said.

There was such heavy sarcasm as to make the speech mean,
"You are lying to me." And this was what Peter felt: coupled

with it was anger at not being believed. He knew Abraham wasn't meant to sound sarcastic, and he felt he somehow had to convince him that he really meant what he said. So Peter found his own words sounding wrong as well – try as he would, he couldn't keep a tone of indignant annoyance out of his voice at being as good as called a liar.

Yes father, with all my heart,
More than anything ever made.

And Abraham's face had an expression on it which said, clearer than words, "That's just how I wanted you to say it," as he continued, with the same heavy sarcasm.

Now who would not be glad that had
A child so loving as thou art?
Your happy face makes me so glad.

And at this the audience laughed. For Peter had felt so nettled that his face looked anything but happy. As he walked off after Abraham had told him to go home to his mother, he felt his ears burning. For he sensed there was little sympathy for him in the audience. "Right cheeky child, that," said a voice in the audience as he stepped up on to the pageant stage. And there was a murmur of agreement; he almost felt they hoped Abraham would kill him.

"You made a mess o'that," said Giles.

"What went wrong?" Peter asked.

"Don't let him rile you," said Gilbert. "Just say your words straight: don't give him the chance he wants – he'll get the whole crowd on his side."

"But how's he doing it?" asked Peter.

"If I were to say to you, 'You're a bright lad,' you'd know it if I meant you were stupid," said Gilbert.

"You're on again," said Giles. "Now, think what you're doing and saying. And keep out of trouble."

Isaac, came a peremptory shout from Abraham.

138

Peter ran out again, back into the sunlight. A muttering from the audience made him feel uncomfortable, unsure of himself. I mustn't let him anger me again, he thought, whatever happens.

Abraham had not lost his sarcasm – as if he was still saying one thing and meaning the opposite. And, of course, for all but a few seconds of the play so far, he had had the audience to himself: he had them on his side already. With meaning glances and winks as well as the tone of voice he had worked up an attitude to Isaac in the audience best described as, "Who's this fool?" It made nonsense of Abraham, nonsense of the play. And somehow Peter had to rise above it.

Look you miss nothing that you will need, said Abraham, telling Isaac what to bring on the expedition.

Make yourself ready, my darling.

Again there was the mocking jeer, this time in the words, "my darling." And once again Peter was stung. But this time he controlled himself. "Sticks and stones may break my bones, but names they cannot hurt me," he muttered defiantly to himself. Aloud, he said, in as quietly dutiful a voice as he could muster:

I am ready to do this deed,
And ever to fulfil your bidding.

Abraham shot him an angry look and continued as before:

My dear son, look thou have no dread;
We shall come home with great loving.

This time it didn't ring quite true – and they both sensed the crowd wasn't so certain it approved of Abraham when Peter's words had sounded so much those of the faithful son. Peter felt a little happier.

After all, he thought, he's banking on my losing my temper. And if I don't, then it's he who's in the mess. Because if he turns nice to me all of a sudden then he can't kill me. He hopes the audience will think that it's a good idea of God's to have me sacrificed. I'll show them it's not.

So he went on, answering Abraham quietly, keeping his temper, keeping control. And as he did so, he saw Abraham's composure slip as anger and frustration took over from sarcasm.

Isaac, he called.

Sir?

Come hither, say I.

Thou shalt be dead, whatsoever betide.

Ah, father. Mercy, Mercy! cried Peter.

Abraham's answer sounded very angry indeed.

What I say may not be denied.

Take your death therefore meekly.

Now there was a definite rumble of anger from the crowd – and now Peter realized that he had turned the tables. Because, if Abraham had been playing his part properly, all his subsequent remarks would have meant, "I can't do anything about this because God has told me to do it." Instead, because he had been so sarcastic and angry, they seemed to mean, "I'm doing this because I mean it." And the quieter and more submissive Peter became, the more he felt the audience moved against Abraham. Abraham felt it too, because he was obviously becoming angrier and angrier. It was he who was losing his temper.

I ask mercy, said Peter.

That may not be, shouted Abraham.

Shall you slay me? Peter said again, quietly.

I know I must, screamed Abraham.

Lie still. I smite.

And at this point, Peter realized, with a sudden sinking of the heart, that he had succeeded too well. Abraham had been pushed over the limit: Peter's quietness and control had made him beside himself with fury. He was quivering with suppressed rage which at any moment would burst out. He's really mad now, thought Peter. He'd slice me up with his sword as soon as look at me. What am I to do?

For Abraham had unsheathed his shining sword, and his eyes seemed to be rolling in his head. Francis and Gyll had spent the morning with their mother in the audience over by the Heaven Pageant. It had been a hard and difficult time for them. They had felt the angry passions of the crowd in the Cain and Abel play. They had kept out of the riot; they had been petrified with fright to see Giles, Gilbert, and Peter in the middle with an angry crowd bearing down on them; they had nearly fainted with shock at seeing Abel "come to life." And though they didn't really understand what was going on, they knew it had to do with Peter and the strange events of the previous days.

They were, of course, very interested in Peter's performance – and realized that, once again, something strange was happening.

"That Parkyn's mad," said Francis.

"He's doing it all wrong," said Gyll. "Peter's making him look a fool."

"He won't like that," said Francis.

"Look," said Gyll. "He's waving his sword. He ought to be making Peter lie down on his face now."

"If Peter's got any sense he'll not let him," said Francis. "The mood he looks to be in, he'd cut him up."

It was obvious Peter had the same thought. For he dodged out of Abraham's way. Then began a crazy chase all round the acting area, Peter running round like a startled rabbit, a maddened Abraham galloping after him. People in the crowd stood up, cheering Peter on: there was no doubt whose side they were on now. Even so, there was also no doubt that this was a real chase – that Abraham was out to kill.

When she looked over to the Abraham and Isaac Pageant, Gyll could see God and an angel carrying a dummy sheep. They were waiting to come on and stop Isaac's sacrifice.

"Look, Francis," she called. "They can't come on till these two stop."

"But they can't stop," said Francis. "Or rather, Peter can't. Abraham will chop him if they do."

"Peter," yelled Gyll at the top of her voice. "Run off t'stage. Come into the audience."

"He can't," said Francis. "He's trying to. But Abraham keeps heading him off."

And then, suddenly, Peter stopped. From where they were, Francis and Gyll could see sweat running down his flushed face. His chest heaved. He stood and faced Abraham. Abraham drew his sword back.

Francis, Gyll, and their mother covered their faces in their hands. They waited. Nothing happened. Then, slowly, Francis raised his head. He could not believe his ears.

Peter was experiencing moments of pure terror. As soon as Abraham had started the chase, Peter's aim had been to escape into the audience. But Abraham must have realized this and showed himself expert at heading off all his ways of escape. He seemed amazingly agile and – for somebody behaving like a violent madman – incredibly clear-minded. The cheers of the crowd swayed round the back of Peter's mind as if they were miles away – almost as if he were lying on a beach listening to the waves. Once or twice he was half-conscious of individual voices he thought he knew. But all this – once again – seemed to be happening to someone else; all he could concentrate on was where to run to next. Each

142

time was the same, until it was like a rhythm; he would blindly stagger on toward the edge of the arena, he would wipe away the blinding sweat from his eyes – and see Abraham in front of him, with his sharp, shining sword.

It's got to stop, it's got to stop: the thought beat round in his head. For his lungs were bursting: he could go no further – there was no chance of pacing himself in this race. But what happens when I do stop? he thought. Soon, he knew, he would have to find out.

It was enough. He could not move another inch. The crowd hushed. He was in the middle of the arena; every eye was on him. He saw Abraham approaching, with slow but measured and purposeful strides. For the second time that day, in spite of the heat, in spite of the sweat which soaked his white tunic, he shivered with hopeless fear.

If only, he thought, if only I could do something – it doesn't matter what. Just something, so as not just to be standing here helpless.

And then, for the second time in three days, something came to his rescue. He suddenly realized that in his pocket was the wooden pipe made by Francis. He didn't remember putting it in his pocket that morning – but he must have, he supposed. So why not play it in these last few seconds? He did; and, over the packed but deathly still arena sounded those high, perky, slightly out-of-tune notes in a jaunty melody which was all Peter knew, though it was totally unlike what he was feeling.

The effect was extraordinary. Abraham stopped. From a place over by the Heaven Pageant the tune was taken up by a similar pipe, and a high voice – Gyll's – called out, "Play away, Peter and Francis." And then, gradually, raggedly, but gathering strength, came the voices of the crowd, singing, chanting, taking up the melody. Now the arena was an inferno of tuneful sound.

Abraham shook his head: he dropped his sword: he stood stock still. His face relaxed. One could not tell if he were coming out of a dream or going into one.

Then, in the middle of all this noise, Peter was aware of another voice.

Abraham, it called. *Abraham.*

The crowd heard it: so too did Abraham. Quiet reigned again: all eyes turned to the Heaven Pageant. And then Peter saw it used properly – the flying-belt for the angels. For, from the top of the Heaven Pageant to the floor beneath he flew – a magnificent angel, in white, his feathery wings like a swan's arching behind his back – and landed lightly, bearing a sheep.

So the play ended – as it should. Abraham sacrificed the sheep and led Isaac off at the close as if all was normal.

But Peter looked into Abraham's eyes and saw that his mind was a million miles away. And when they had walked back on to the pageant and after Peter had sat down and closed his eyes for a moment in utter exhaustion, he opened them to find that Abraham had slipped away and was nowhere to be seen.

— 15 —

SHEPHERDS

Peter wanted quiet: he walked off the pageant and lay down in the grass some way from the acting arena. He needed a rest: he was shaking from the horrible fright he had received. He stretched out, feeling the hot sun on his face.

Before he knew what had happened, he was asleep.

When he woke up, the sun had shifted round in the sky so that it was now almost directly overhead. He was conscious of a raging thirst. And then he realized they were all – Gilbert, Giles, his wife, Francis, and Gyll – bending over him.

"Eh, lad," said Giles. "We've been looking all over for thee."

"We should have let him sleep on," said Gilbert. "There's time before t' Shepherds."

"Nay, Gilbert. T'lad's well earnt his shilling this day," said Giles. "Let him watch for t'rest of day."

"No," said Peter. "I've got to do the Shepherds' play – and there can't be anything in it like the last one. I can keep out of trouble."

"By God's bones, lad, tha ran it close with yon Parkyn," said Giles.

"He'll have to do it," said Gilbert. "Because he know's what's what and there's no one else does."

"I've brought thee a bowl of water," said Giles's wife.

At least one person knows what's important, thought Peter as he drank great gulps out of the wooden bowl and sluiced his face and neck with what was left.

"And some oat cakes for thee," she continued.

Peter gratefully ate them: he hadn't realized what a great pit of hunger there was in his stomach until that moment.

Much refreshed, he asked what had been going on.

"While tha's been snoring thy head off here," said Giles, "There's been t'Jacob play, t'Prophets' play, Pharaoh, and Caesar Augustus. We're coming up to t'Shepherd's play soon. We've done twelve plays; 'tis noon now and when tha've done wi' shepherds there'll be sixteen left. So dark will be near on us when t'finish of day comes."

"Any more trouble?" asked Peter.

"Nay. 'Tis as we thought," said Giles. "'Tis only the plays as the fellows we know of are in where wrong things happen."

"Have you seen the Ancient?" asked Peter.

"Him!" laughed Giles. "He'll not show his face here now. You get us through t'Shepherds' play, lad, and t'day's at an end."

"Be not so sure, Giles Doleffe," said Gilbert. "I had a dream."

"A dream!" scoffed Giles. "There'd need to be more than a dream and an old man in a ragged cloak to keep us from being a step ahead of these carls."

"'Tis time, Peter," said Gilbert, ignoring Giles's remark. "Time for thy last performance in these plays."

146

They all walked over to the Shepherds' Pageant, except Gyll, Francis and their mother, who went back to their place. Peter found that he was actively looking forward to this play: nothing could scare him now after what he had been through, he thought. A little warning voice inside him told him he might be rejoicing too soon, but he tried not to listen to it.

There was a setback, however, almost at once. When they entered the changing-room, the first thing they saw was a boy, a little older than Peter, dressed in a green smock and holding a shepherd's crook.

"I've not seen thee these few days, Master Giles," he said. "Wheer's tha been?"

Giles reddened with embarrassment while Gilbert exploded.

"Tha great lump, Giles Doleffe. I told thee to tell him. Tha said tha would."

"'Tis a worrisome day, Gilbert," said Giles awkwardly. "I forgot."

"Then tell him now," roared Gilbert.

Peter, too, felt very embarrassed. Giles cleared his throat and shifted uneasily on his feet.

"Peter here is playing thy part today," he said. "I meant to tell thee."

"Him? Him as was Isaac? A right mess he made of that. I'll not let him do my part."

"If 'tis all to come to naught because of thee, Giles," said Gilbert, "thou'lt have much to answer for."

"Now look here, lad," said Giles to the boy. "I'm Pageant Master and what I say goes. There's good reason for this: I'll pay thee well to keep out of it – and t'part is thine for next year."

It's been a day of promises for Giles, thought Peter.

At this point four other people entered. One, Peter presumed, was Mak: another was Gyll, his wife. He did not have to be told who the others were: he had seen the two older shepherds before on two occasions now. So Giles's humiliation had a large audience.

"All right," said the boy, to the surprise of all of them. "I'll take thee at thy word."

"That's right good of thee, lad," said Giles, almost sweating with relief.

"But have a care for the rest of the day," said the boy with a meaning glance at Peter, which made him feel very uncomfortable. And then he left the pageant.

"See that?" said Giles. "I tell thee, Gilbert, I've a way with people that makes them do as I say wi' no fuss. There's no need to worry."

"That's not like him at all to give in so easy," said Gilbert. "Watch out for afterwards, Peter."

"Are we ready?" said Giles.

"Nay, Master Giles," said Mak. "T'other shepherds have gone with him."

It was true. They had slipped out after the boy and were nowhere to be seen.

"We'll be late starting," moaned Giles. "And 'tis best play, is this."

"I'll go after them," said Mak.

"I don't like this," said Gilbert. "Why should they go? What do they want with t'lad?"

Almost immediately Mak entered with the two shepherds – who both slouched sluggishly as had Abraham.

"Stop thy worrying," said Giles. "We are ready."

There was no doubt about it; Peter enjoyed every moment of the Shepherds' play. Coll and Gyb, the two old shepherds, gave no sign that anything was wrong. The audience was relaxed and happy; the violence of the morning seemed to be forgotten. They warmed quickly to the shepherds, Peter included. He was now so confident of himself that he felt nothing could go wrong. All the business with the stolen sheep in the cradle went perfectly; the audience roared with laughter exactly where they felt they should; when the shepherds appeared to have left Mak's house without the sheep there were frenzied shouts of "Go back," "'Tis there," "Don't believe that Mak." And Peter smiled to listen to them.

But – as he had thought on the very first day – the crowd was very doubtful about Mak himself. Was he funny? Was he serious? Was he a threat? Was he a magician? The people seemed to be holding back somehow when he was on the stage. And when, near the end, the shepherds had found the sheep, Peter felt a very definite surge of hostility toward Mak.

It was Peter who pulled the sheep out of the cradle, thinking it was a baby.

Let me give him a kiss, he said.

I'll lift up the clout.

What the devil is this? he's got a great long snout.

He's marked amiss, said Coll, *We'll not wait about.*

Ill-spun weft, said Gyb, *always comes foul out.*

Ah, so.

He's just like our sheep.

How, Gyb? said Peter. *May I peep?*

The noise from the people was hard to fathom. Just like the shepherds, they were angry but amused at the same time.

But it was now that Peter remembered why he was there; he remembered Gilbert had seen these same two shepherds chase Mak down the street as if to lynch him; he remembered how they had stood, dark and menacing in the dovecote. And he said to himself, "This is it."

It was his turn to speak.

Let's burn this woman, and tie her up fast
And this false Mak will hang at the last.

The words were out before he could call them back. He'd never really thought what they meant before. You fool, he raged inwardly. Why hadn't you noticed those words until now? It's *you* who egg them on to killing Mak, when you're supposed to be out here to stop it.

The next words he faltered over, though they were important –

Will you see how they swaddle
His four feet in the middle?
I never saw in a cradle
A horned lad before.

But nobody listened. It was as if his words had opened a floodgate of action. Anger had triumphed over amusement in the minds of the crowd – and the two elder shepherds acted on it. To Peter's horror they both produced ropes from under their smocks: Gyb pinioned Gyll and moved her over to her stage house, obviously to tie her up to one of the posts which held the roof up, while – and this caused a gasp from everyone – Coll brandished a huge noose and moved toward Mak menacingly. The audience roared its approval.

In vain, Peter shouted out the lines he really understood:

I know a better way to show them.
We'll not take an eye for an eye
Nor string them up high,
But up in a canvas we'll throw them.

Nobody listened: nobody even heard. Gilbert was right, Peter thought. I am the tiger let in the gates. It's all happening because of me. And he hid his head in his hands for a moment in despair. But then he thought again; I'll have to stop them myself. So he straightened up and wondered whose rescue he should go to first.

Then he saw he had an ally. Mak's wife was not going to be tied up. She was very big – too strong, in fact, for Gyb. She knocked him aside and produced a knife. She'll stab him, Peter thought – but she did not. She merely seized his rope and cut it into as many pieces as she could. And while Gyb stood looking stupidly and helpless at the bit of frayed rope round him, she ran over to where Mak and Coll were fighting. Coll was winning; he had got the noose over Mak's head and was trying to drag him over to the pageant itself. But Mak's wife leapt in, sliced the rope through just above the noose – and Mak was free.

"Now canst tha do it?" she yelled at Coll. "I'll teach thee."

Then she turned to Peter.

"Don't stand there like a lump, lad," she roared. "Say thy words again."

So, still nonplussed, Peter repeated what he had just said.

. . . *and up in a canvas we'll throw them*, he ended, rather lamely, thinking nothing would happen. To his surprise, Coll and Gyb seemed now perfectly amenable. They were quite happy to help Peter throw Mak and his wife up in the blanket: when they were finished, Mak's wife gasped to Peter, "There's been queer things happening: best to be ready for owt. I thought tha'd not be helping me."

"I nearly didn't," said Peter, feeling rather puzzled.

Meanwhile, the play continued, with Coll and Gyb behaving as though nothing had happened and the audience – now probably incapable of being surprised by anything – giving attention and interest as close as ever.

Another angel descended and told them to go to the manger. They did so – and for a fleeting moment Peter wondered if the manger might in fact be empty. That would cause a sensation and, as it was Giles's responsibility to make sure it wasn't, one couldn't be quite sure – after all, thought Peter, it doesn't seem to be his day!

But all went well: the ending of the play was uneventful. After giving their gifts, the shepherds ran off – Peter, as always, back to Gilbert and Giles.

"Well done, lad," said Giles. "Tha did it. That's t'finish then."

Suddenly, a wave of regret swept through Peter. "I suppose it is," he said. "The plays are over. I've done what I came for."

"And we won," said Giles.

Gilbert was silent.

"It doesn't seem right," said Peter. "What I did wasn't worth coming back five hundred years for."

"What dost tha mean?" said Giles.

"That Shepherds' play was a shambles in the middle. And it was Mak's wife who got us out of the mess. I didn't. I nearly got us into it because I didn't know what I was saying."

"Tha were right good as Isaac," said Giles, "Tha stopped yon fellow in his tracks there all right."

"I didn't," said Peter. "I was scared stiff. I don't know what came over me to blow my pipe. I didn't do anything special, like Abel. All right, things look as if they've gone well. There aren't any more dodgy plays. But it doesn't seem worthwhile dragging me back all this way for what I've done. Anybody could have done it – and a lot better than I did, too."

For the first time, Gilbert spoke. "The day is not yet over," he said.

The sun went in, quite suddenly. A cloud passed over it: when they looked up, they saw that more were following. Far away, toward the horizon, was a bank of thick black cloud.

"The sunshine and the warmth are nearly over," said Gilbert. "But as for this day, it is not yet over."

"Tha'll not believe a good thing when tha sees it," said Giles. "What art tha speaking of?"

"Would that I knew," said Gilbert. "We have not played through to the end of my dream. We have avoided disasters on the way, but we have not come to the end."

"By God, tha talkest some right strange stuff," said Giles. "Art tha going to watch rest o' t' plays, then? There's some more o' thine still to be done."

So, as the afternoon wore on, Peter sat with Gilbert and Giles on the grass between the Shepherds pageant and the seats and watched the plays continue. He watched the Magi, the flight into Egypt – and then the play of Herod the Great, which Gilbert had written. There followed the plays of Christ's life, culminating in the scourging and buffeting (more of Gilbert's work here), and then the Crucifixion itself. And at this point, Peter felt quite sure that Gilbert was wrong and Giles was right, that nothing more would happen, that they had in fact won. For the audience was quiet, intent, rapt. The plays were having the effect they were intended to have. All things were moving to their pre-ordained end: Peter could easily see these people living another year in relative peace and as near happiness as the awful poverty of their surroundings would allow, because the message, "It's all right; you can keep going until the plays next year" was coming over loud and clear – to him as much as to everybody else.

The play of the Ascension would soon be starting; only the Judgment play was to follow. It was now evening. It had grown dark very quickly: the bank of cloud had covered the sky. It was close, humid: rumbles of thunder could be heard in the distance. Peter began to feel almost suffocated.

"I'm going for a walk," he said to Gilbert. "I won't be more than a minute."

Gilbert nodded. Peter went through to the back of the pageant – and as he turned to walk across the grass he was without warning seized hard from behind. His arms were caught and twisted and a knee came up into the small of his back.

"Gilbert!" he shouted at the top of his voice.

"I'll stop this row," said a slightly familiar voice. It was, Peter realized after a moment, the boy who should have played Daw, the third shepherd. He shoved a large, dirty, and hard hand over Peter's mouth and pushed him forward. "I'll not thump thee meself," he said. "I'll take thee to them as makes a better job of it than I can. They'll be pleased to see thee."

Peter struggled: but the boy was far too strong for him. Nobody saw as Peter was forced round the back of the seats to the other side of the arena. Nobody saw as they approached the bulk of the Hell Pageant, or so Peter thought. But then he heard footsteps behind them and a voice, calling, "Peter, Peter!"

It's Gilbert, thought Peter. He heard me shout.

However, the door at the back of the Hell Pageant was open: the boy pushed Peter through it. As he picked himself up and his eyes grew used to the semi-darkness, his first thought was that he was back where he started. Now he knew why the two elder shepherds had slipped out after Daw before the play.

For there in front of him stood the whole crew – Cain, Abraham, Coll, and Gyb.

And with them stood the Ancient.

— 16 —

THE FINAL MEETING

The same face; the same wrinkles, bones, and parchment skin; the same sooty, mildewed monk's habit; the same spreading all round of an atmosphere of cold, damp futility; by now Peter knew them all with an awful familiarity.

For a while there was silence, then a sudden bumping and a gasping for breath indicated that Gilbert had clumped his way into the room and subsided on to the floor, panting hard just by the door.

"They are both here," said the same distant voice. "Both here and thinking I was beaten."

The five henchmen stood still, their faces unmoving. The Ancient's eyes turned to Gilbert.

"But what eyes did you see in the dream that was sent you? And when did they appear? Who blew the horn? Soon you will know."

Gilbert groaned aloud.

"So somehow you kept your plays today on an even keel," went on the Ancient. "But what will happen when the devil with the horn appears in lightning and thunder and blows his summons to the world? What will happen when the miserable flock outside scatters in fear? What will happen when they turn and see ranged around them fiends upon fiends, like sheepdogs, pushing them back, back, back – funnelling them down on Hell mouth, till they pass in a great stream through its doors? And what will they do when the jaws clamp down after the last one is through?"

There was a heavy rumble of thunder from outside.

"I sent you a dream, Master Gilbert," continued the Ancient in a quieter voice. "I sent you a dream which made you cudgel your brains for a meaning. And you – and your actors – nearly foiled my design. But why should I not let you? Why should not I let the little fool from the future have his brief moment of fear and glory? Why should I not tease you when I can give you a riddling hint and take it away from you in the moment of your puny triumph just as I choose to?

"Master Gilbert, in your dream you saw the crowd rise up and run, into the town; and all around you saw the fires started, the crying of those trampled under foot and the crying of those who were killed. You heard the shout of 'Our God has gone away.' It has haunted you ever since in your mind. And in only a very few minutes you will see it and hear it in reality, for all round you it will be happening."

Again, Gilbert groaned.

A slow pale burst of lightning briefly illuminated the tiny, half-dark room. Peter saw the Ancient was carrying what looked like a red suit of clothes. Even as the lightning died away, he slipped off the black habit, revealing a skeletal, derelict body which, Peter noticed with a shock, was as far decomposed as that in the painting in the Chantry Bridge Chapel. At once, though, the Ancient began to pull on the red clothes, which seemed to be a devil's costume just like those in the box which Peter had already seen.

But, to his horror, amazement, and stupefaction, there was a change before his eyes which defied explanation. The Ancient did not put the clothes on in any ordinary sense – he seemed somehow to grow them. And what resulted was not just a devil of the sort that could caper round the room making up rhymes but something which Peter's eyes could not take in. For as he watched, the shape appeared to grow vast: too big for the little room, the walls of which seemed to disappear into nothingness until it was as if they were all suspended in space. And the eyes grew larger, redder, until Peter could not bear to look at them. Before him now stood a devilish shape out of a nightmare. And then he knew that in truth Gilbert's dream was coming true.

Gilbert realized it too. He was covering his face with his hands and uttering great wordless cries of anguish. Peter was powerless to move, transfixed with horror. Everything seemed, in the light emanating from this creature, bathed in a fiery, lurid glow: it seemed they were far away in time and place from the little dressing-room at the back of the Hell Pageant at Goodybower in Dunfield.

And still the four henchmen of the Ancient – Cain, Abraham, Coll, and Gyb – stood silent, waiting.

Now the creature spoke again: no longer with the high distant voice of the Ancient but deeply, so that the noise seemed to reverberate inside the mind – and Peter remembered Gilbert's previous description of it.

"Now take good heed, Master Gilbert. Who shall I have for my sheepdogs? I have four here whom you know and who have served me well today although you bested them. But I have one who serves *you*, who came back a long way with you and who should by now be back where he comes from. But why send him back home when I can use him? How frightened you were when you saw him dressed in devil's skin and you wondered if he was not my minion after all. Well, he was, and is, and shall be for evermore."

Peter realized it was he the creature was talking of; he summoned up just enough mental energy to realize that the Ancient had been playing with them all the time; that Gilbert had feared this all along; that there was nothing that could now be done to avert the catastrophe at the end of Gilbert's dream. Then he felt his will drain away; he knew he was no more than the creature's slave.

"Put on your costumes," the creature ordered.

Somehow they must have been still in the dressing-room after all because Abraham and Coll bent down and opened up a box full of devil's clothes. Awkwardly, because the room was so very small, all five of them – for Peter felt a strange certainty and compulsion that he had to – pulled on the hot, heavy costumes and stood huddled together, waiting for the creature to speak.

"Now I will rise to the top of the pageant. I will blow the horn long and loud. The people will start up in terror. Hell mouth will open. You will run out and head the whole flock off, back into the arena, and through the mouth of Hell."

And even as they watched he seemed to disappear.

Now thunder rolled, lightning flashed all round. Above the thunder sounded the notes of the horn; two long, high, clear notes, notes which seemed to say, "Turn and look at me, for I am your fate."

Then, creakingly, but inexorably, though there was nobody on the winch, Hell mouth opened; a blast of cold air came down it, but little light, for the sky was black with cloud and riven with thunder and lightning. But there was a glimpse of a small segment of the rows of intent white faces outside.

As if in a dream, as if dead men, as if ghosts, Peter and the other four shuffled up the passage through Hell mouth, jostling and bumping each other, for the way was narrow. They passed the carious, blood-bespattered teeth and the mutilated bodies wedged between them and then out into the open air, to perform the last act of the day.

– 17 –

CONCLUSIONS

Like everybody else, Francis, Gyll, and their mother had enjoyed the pageants much more after the Shepherds' Play was over. All danger seemed past: the day was progressing as it always had – the greatest day of the year, not excepting Christmas, and better than ever this year because of Gilbert's new plays.

Even when the sky had started to cloud over and thunder began to rumble distantly, they had felt no urge to move away.

"T'storm will hold off till after t'plays," said their mother, "'Tis only once a year, is this."

There seemed to be a very long wait after the Play of the Ascension.

"'Tis only t'Judgement Play to come," said Francis. "What's stopping it?"

The sky was even darker now. A wind played round the flags and the loose clothes of the audience that was really quite cold. The thunder rumbled intermittently – but gradually became louder. The gaps between the pale lightning and the rollings of thunder became smaller. Nobody in the

160

crowd left: but people were becoming restive; mutterings and shoutings were breaking out everywhere.

"Hey, here comes Tuttivillus," said Gyll suddenly – and indeed there seemed to be some sort of movement on the top of Hell Pageant.

They waited.

Then, with an indrawn rush of terrified breath, people stopped their ears and hid their eyes. For the awful sound assaulted them; a high-pitched squeal boring into their ears – and there, in a sheet of flame on the top of the Hell Pageant, they saw him, a great bulk, formless but terrifying, fearful eyes burning, blowing his horn in a summons to them all, which said somehow to each individual person there, "I want you in here."

There were screams and shouts of terror in the crowd: many turned and tried to blunder their way out of the arena. Francis and his mother turned to go as well, but Gyll, her face troubled with many conflicting thoughts, said, "No; stay if you can bear it."

For she had seen the mouth of Hell opening and she thought she knew what might come out of it. Her mind flew back to the night she had searched for Peter: her fears, her doubts, the things she had seen, the things she had thought. She remembered her wonderings about Peter – and especially his shoes, which still worried her. And she remembered how she had seen him capering round the Hell Pageant dressed as a devil, and how Gilbert – who knew better than any of them – had gone nearly berserk at the sight. So she at least half-expected what was to come out of the mouth of Hell.

A long burst of lightning gave an unearthly glow to the five red, repulsive figures who stood close together on the stage in front of Hell. Gyll's mother gave a scream and hid her eyes.

"No, mother. One of them is Peter. I know it," cried Gyll.

At the sight of these new horrors – which to the people seemed totally and disturbingly different from the little capering devils they laughed at every year in the Judgement Play, especially while the unearthly din reverberated in their ears – the cries and shouts redoubled. There was chaos as the crowd turned, pushed and panicked its way out of the arena, huddling in frightened groups close to the gaps between the rakes of seats. Great cracking noises sounded as seats began to collapse and break, and there were shouts and howls of pain from those who fell.

But Gyll kept watching the five. And what she saw next defied everything she had expected.

For the group began to split up. She guessed they were going to fan out round the crowd as soon as they could.

But something quite extraordinary seemed to be happening. The devils appeared stuck to the ground. The one on the right ran out one way; the devil next to him fell over. The first devil stopped as if he had run into a wall and promptly sat down. The devil on the far left, who was by far the biggest, also stopped after he had run for three feet. But he did not fall. He strained hard – and somehow appeared to be pulling the other four along with him.

One of the devils tried to dash out suddenly into the middle, like a sprinter. But his stopping was so violent that he fell head over heels and fetched up a twitching heap on the ground.

Realizing something was wrong, the devils seemed to blame each other. One turned and aimed a blow at another's head: in a few minutes, instead of being terrible demons striking fear into the hearts of all, there was a heaving, scrambling mass of red-clothed, obviously human bodies.

Gyll watched amazed for a while; then she began to laugh and laugh and laugh. Francis looked at the devils, and then joined in with her laughter. Their mother forgot her fear and laughed too. The sound was heard by others who stopped in their flight and looked – and laughed as well. And gradually, over the whole of the arena, panic ceased as everybody turned to look; laughter, wave upon wave of it, took its place, echoing all over, filling the air and reaching to the heavens. The shape on the Hell Pageant had disappeared. Gilbert stirred at the back of the pageant: got up and came to see what caused this unexpected noise. And he saw the heaving, angry mass of red-clothed devils and – mystified though he was – he laughed too.

Gyll wiped the tears from her eyes. She felt weak and limp. She looked at Francis.

"What's to do?" he said.

"'Tis that Peter," she said. "He forgot to untie t'devils' tails."

Peter was at the very bottom of this heavy pile, feeling nearly squashed to death, when he too remembered the only possible explanation for what was happening. He managed to free his head to shout, above the laughter all round him, "Get off. The tails are tied together."

"Yer what?" came a voice from inside the heap. Gradually the devils pulled themselves apart. One fumbled in his costume and brought out a knife.

"Wheer's t'knot, then?" he said.

"Here," said Peter, lifting up the great wodge of wooden stings.

The devil cut the knot, the tails all fell noisily to the wooden floor and one devil said, "I'm tekkin' this lot off."

They all did, and once again Peter saw the faces of Cain, Abraham, Coll, and Gyb.

"Hey, Parkyn," said Coll. "I never knew thee was in t'Judgement Play."

"I'm not, Jack Gibbon," said Abraham. "I've no notion what this lot's doing on me."

"Same here," said Cain. "Wheer's me brother?"

And then Peter realized that whatever had before afflicted them was gone; gone for ever.

"Right funny rehearsal this has been," said Gyb. "I come here as a shepherd and go as a devil."

"But the plays are over," said Peter.

"Don't be daft," said Abraham. "And anyroad, who art thou?"

Peter realized they had all come out of a dream.

"You'll know soon enough," he said.

And then it began to rain; soon the storm was washed away out of the sky.

There was feasting in the little town that night; sheep and oxen were roasted whole on spits in the streets; the ale flowed free. Giles – whom Peter had not seen for hours – was happier than Peter thought possible. His children and wife tried hard to make Peter go out with them into the street, where the fires and torches lit up the spire of the great church in the darkness and moving shadows in thousands followed the milling people around.

"Why not come?" asked Francis.

Peter did not answer. He found that he was losing interest in it all. He sensed it was time for him to go home. But there were still explanations to be made.

"Peter," said Gyll. "Why dost tha wear t' Devil's shoes?"

The look on her face made it seem as if she had had to force herself to ask the question.

"What are you talking about?"

"There's devil's stitching on them. And they leave the Devil's footmarks. 'Tis like if tha puts foot to t'ground 'tis his hoofprint is left."

164

Peter laughed. "But you can buy them anywhere where – where I come from."

"Where is that?" asked Gyll quietly.

Where do I start? thought Peter. "Gilbert will tell you," he said lamely.

"But thou'rt not afeared of him. So tha must *know* him."

"Who?"

"The Devil."

"Why say I'm not afraid of him? I was scared stiff in the plays," said Peter.

"All the tails were tied together by thee," said Gyll. "What we feared you made us laugh at. So he were beaten. But you have his shoes, and thou'rt not afeard of him. So surely tha knows him."

"Gilbert must have thought the same when he saw me dressed up that day in the Hell Pageant," said Peter. "No wonder he shouted."

"Thou'rt a puzzle to me, Peter," said Gyll. "T' Devil is all there is to fear. But thou'rt not afeard of him. Yet thou art afeard o' summat – tha said so."

"It's not the same thing at all," said Peter.

"It must be," said Gyll.

"Come on," said Francis. "We'll get nowt to eat else."

Francis and Gyll ran off. As Peter watched them go, the wish to return to his own time became overpowering. When Gilbert entered the room at that moment, he said so to him.

"I know," was the answer. "Thy real clothes are still in the bundle, which is by my bed. Slip them on, and the robe I gave thee over the top of it. Then we will go."

In a few minutes, Peter was ready, his twentieth-century clothes feeling unfamiliar and heavy on him.

"Where to?" he asked.

"Back along the Doncaster Road," said Gilbert.

Peter carefully made sure that the pipe Francis had given him was tightly gripped in his hand; it will be a marvellous souvenir, he thought.

"Let's go, then," he said.

They walked unnoticed through the revelling crowds. Peter saw sights which gladdened his heart; the shepherds and Abraham with their families, laughing and happy; Abel and his big brother storming round the streets singing and waving their jugs of ale. But he never saw Giles, his wife, Francis, or Gyll. They went past Kergate Bar again, through the trees, and on to the open road leading down to the River Calder.

Now it was dark and quiet. Clouds obscured the moon. Peter spoke.

"Say goodbye to the others for me," he said.

"I will," said Gilbert.

"Is it all really finished?" asked Peter. "Is your dream over?"

"It will never be really over," said Gilbert. "But this we can say: if the battle is ever lost, it was not lost here today."

"Listen," said Peter.

The sound of the waters of the Calder could be heard; they were approaching the bridge.

And then the moon came out.

"Look ahead," breathed Peter.

In the moonlight before them they could see it, just moving on to the bridge; the silhouette of a thin, cloaked figure, trudging with a staff away from the town; hunched, dogged, like a bat with no life in its wings. They both knew at once who it was. They stopped and watched him cross the bridge, to be lost to sight in the trees on the other side.

"There's nowt left for him here," said Gilbert. "But he'll be back, somewhere, sometime."

166

They walked on. They reached the bridge; before them loomed the pinnacled bulk of the Chantry Chapel.

"I'll be going in here for a while," said Gilbert. "When I come out, I expect tha'll be gone."

And Peter knew that he would be.

He held out his hand to Gilbert, who grasped it firmly.

"Goodbye, lad," he said. "Tha've done well. I thank thee for it."

He opened the door of the chapel and went inside, disappearing from Peter's view.

For a moment or two, Peter stood irresolute, wondering what to do and what would happen, but keeping a tight grip on the little wooden pipe. Then, just as before, it was as if he was swept off his feet and caught up in the air. But, even as he was swirled between the centuries, the wooden pipe crumbled away to dust in his hand.

– 18 –

DUNFIELD

The violent jerking of the train as it came to a halt made Peter's eyes open. He blinked in the compartment's bright, artificial light. Outside it was dark – but not the black, impenetrable darkness he had been lately used to. He saw roads far below them, lined with street lamps and busy with cars. For a strange moment, he thought the train was hovering in mid-air.

"Aye, we're stopped on t'viaduct," said a voice.

With a shock, Peter realized a man was sitting where Gilbert had been – was it only a few hours ago?

"Where are we?" he said.

"Just outside Dunfield Station – on t'viaduct, like I said. Eh, tha's had a good sleep, lad. I'm not surprised – a right bad run this has been."

"What's been bad about it?"

"Eh, how long has tha been asleep, then? We're two hours late. Didn't you know train broke down south of Newark and relief engine had to come out to pull you in? It's near on seven o'clock."

"I must have slept all through it," said Peter.

168

"By heck, you were well away when I got on at Don-caster. I reckon Ossett town band wouldn't have woken you."

An impatient blast on the engine's horn echoed in the night air.

"It were funny seeing you wake up like that," said the man. "It reminded me of a mate o'mine who were in a train stopped by signals on t'viaduct one night – it were some time ago now, because it were in a carriage with doors on each side. There were a chap sitting opposite fast asleep, just like you were, and he suddenly woke up, shouted 'We're here,' picked up his case, opened t'door and walked straight out. Ee, my mate were right shocked I can tell you. Anyway, this chap, he climbed back in t'train, all cut and bruised and shaken, still clutching his case, and he says, 'Ee, I am a right fool,' he says. 'I got out wrong side o' t'train.' And he opened t'door on t'other side and walked straight out of that. Well, train started then, and he never heard what happened to him. What do you think of that, then?"

Before Peter had a chance to say what he thought of it, the connecting door slid open and the ticket-collector appeared.

"Ah, woken up, have you?" he said. "Here we are in Dun-field, then. I said I'd see you off the train all right."

So he did, thought Peter. How long ago was it?

Slowly the train groped its way across the viaduct and drew into Dunfield Station. Peter opened his case and pulled out his blue quilted anorak. He slipped it on, pulled up the zip, and then stuffed his magazines, which were still open on the table, back into the case and closed it.

"Goodbye, then," said the man who had told him the story, "I'm going on to Leeds. Have a good Christmas."

"I hope you do too. Goodbye," said Peter as he stood up and walked down the center gangway. He was surprised to find that he felt stiff, as if he were not used to using his legs.

The ticket-collector was already at the door. He had pushed the window down ready to turn the handle outside. The train ground to a halt as the freezing night air blew in on Peter's face. The door was opened.

"Thank you. Goodbye," said Peter, and stepped on to the platform.

All the clouds were gone. The sky was ablaze with stars; moonlight gave great help to the station lamps. Peter stood still, his bag at his feet, as people swirled all around him.

His journey was over.

It was mid-morning on the following day; still cold, clear, and frosty. Peter was walking the streets of Dunfield, on his own amid a hurrying, bustling crowd of people. All the time remembrances assailed him; the directions he was taking seemed familiar, though the surroundings never did – until he turned a corner. Suddenly, there was the great church – now sadly dirty and soot-stained, but reminding him keenly of how he had last seen it. Though alien in its new surroundings, hemmed in by roads with Marks and Spencer on one side and the higgledy back entrances of shops on the other, its sight made him stop in his tracks.

And nearly every face he saw seemed oddly familiar; the set of a mouth, the tilt of a nose, the curve of an eyebrow – all these things would recall the faces of the ancient ancestors he had walked and talked with so recently. Somewhere deep in his mind, as he saw strange connections between then and now, there were tears for the loss of friends he could never conceivably meet again; for Gilbert, his guide, wise and far seeing; for Giles, who had forced him to do things he thought he could not; for Francis, who had been his friend, in spite of all; and for Gyll, who had tried to understand him and had choked back her fears to rescue him. And what if she had not? thought Peter. Would the tingling air which now invigorated him have felt instead like the clammy numbness which had exuded from the body of the Ancient? Would he have felt suffocated by the crowd all round him, instead of being enlivened, as he was. For he shared with all these people as they went about their pre-Christmas business a happiness and expectancy which he knew he had a right to feel. Here were no zombies, no walking dead. The Ancient was wrong – had been defeated. Side by side with regret for his lost companions was a feeling of delight, even of triumph.

Peter had been glad to reach the house of his uncle and aunt the previous night. The huge plate of egg, sausage, and chips and the cups of tea they had ready for him had tasted better than he could have imagined. But beneath the warmth and comfort was the nagging question; what news from home?

The telephone had not rung for a very long time – but when it did, Peter reached it in a split-second, his heart racing.

"Yes, your mother will be all right," his father had said. "She's out of danger."

I have to ask this, thought Peter. "Did she nearly die?"

"We're very lucky," was the answer. "It was close. I can't believe she's pulled through so quickly. But the doctors seem sure."

And they're right to be, thought Peter. I know it.

"Have they caught the ones who did it?" he asked.

"No." His father's voice sounded less happy. "And what's the point? If they do, there'll be more where they came from."

For a second, Peter had a mental picture of an ancient, wrinkled face, its cheeks caved in with what could have been a mocking smile.

"Don't say that," he had said.

"Stay up there for a few days," said his father. "Enjoy yourself. You can now."

And I will, thought Peter as he walked the streets. For it had ended. His unlooked-for quest was over. His own struggle had helped that of his mother unconscious in a hospital bed. They had won.

A sensation of total contentment stole over him. So much had happened – and now there was so much to look forward to. His mother, weak at first but quickly convalescing, to come home. Two Christmasses. Another train journey – and this time, he hoped, hauled by a Deltic, with not an inch of the line between Dunfield and King's Cross to be missed.

And when he reached home, there was "Evening Star" to be finished.

AUTHOR'S NOTE

Dunfield does exist. That's not its real name, of course. If you want to know that, you must find out where the King's Cross–Leeds express stops after Doncaster. In the nineteenth century a novelist was born in the town whose name was George Gissing. He wrote a novel called *A Life's Morning* which is about his birthplace. He called the town in the book "Dunfield"; I thought it seemed – if his ghost would not mind – a good name to take over.

Miracle Plays were performed there; the plays mentioned in this book are very slightly adapted from them. The plays as a whole are often called *The Towneley Cycle*. (Why *Towneley* is another story.)

There was such a person as Gilbert (though whether that was his name is very doubtful). Certainly, one man wrote all the plays Gilbert says are his. But who was he? Nobody knows. He is often called "The Master" – somebody once had a theory he was called Gilbert de Pilkington. I don't know if it's true (personally I doubt it) – but Gilbert seemed a good name to give "The Master" in this book.

Giles Doleffe really lived as well. He was a draper by trade – and a Pageant Master who kept a copy of the plays in his own house. But he and "The Master" could never have met in real life, for Giles lived a century afterwards. Giles had a wife, but I don't know about his children.

There are shops and a covered market now where the quarry at Goodybower used to be. But you can see the great church – now a cathedral – with its spire; and you can see the Chantry Chapel on the bridge over the Calder.

There was a dovecote, but traces of it long ago disappeared. However, if you want to see a dovecote *something* like the one I've described, you'll find it at Willington in Bedfordshire – though this one was not built until the sixteenth century.

A word about the way the plays are performed. You may have read or been told that miracle plays were performed on carts which were towed around from place to place so that each play was performed several times a day. For a long time I thought the same.

However, over the last twenty years, many scholars and men of the theatre have done much research and have shown that a system something like that which is described in this book is at least as likely to have been used. Personally, I am very glad. I have always thought the plays were far too good for the backs of carts. I like the idea of the central arena, like a circus ring, a bull-ring, or the Centre Court at Wimbledon, as a setting for the plays. The people of the Middle Ages may not have had much, but anybody who looks at the way they built their cathedrals surely can't believe they would be content to put their plays on the backs of carts.

In case you think that the events at the end of the book are a little too far-fetched, just remember that it is recorded that at the end of the sixteenth century a performance of *Dr Faustus,* a play by Christopher Marlowe about the man who sold his soul to the devil, broke up in confusion. Both actors and audience ran away in fear because *an extra devil had appeared on the stage and nobody could account for him.*

So think on.

There are a lot of books now about Miracle Plays – far too many to mention here. However, below are the names of a few which gave me help in writing this story.

The Towneley Cycle – (The Early English Text Society); All the Wakefield plays in the original Middle English.

The Wakefield Mystery Plays – edited and translated by Martial Rose (Evans).

Three Towneley Plays – adapted with introduction by Dennis Hamley (Heinemann Educational Books).

The Medieval Theatre in the Round – Richard Sothern.

The Seven Ages of the Theatre – Richard Sothern (Faber).

English Drama from the Earliest times to the Elizabethans – A. P. Rossitter (Hutchinson).

Early English Stages. Vol. 1 (1300–1576) – Glynne Wickham (R. & K. P.).

Drama and Religion in the English Mystery Plays – Eleanor Prosser (Stanford University Press).

Medieval Drama – A. M. Kinghorn (Evans).

The Wakefield Pageants in the Towneley Cycle – edited by A. C. Cawley (Manchester University Press).

Dennis Hamley

ABOUT THE AUTHOR

Dennis Hamley was born in 1935 in Kent, England. He read English at Cambridge University and worked for many years as a teacher, a teacher-trainer, and an adviser to schools. He also founded the *Lending Our Minds Out* creative writing courses for children. In 1992 he turned to writing full-time. *Pageants of Despair* was his first novel. His latest novel, *Ellen's People,* is set in the First World War and has recently been published in the UK. In between, he wrote more than fifty other books, including *Spirit of the Place, Out of the Mouths of Babes,* and the Joslin de Lay Mysteries series, set, like *Pageants of Despair,* in the Middle Ages. Hamley now lives in Hertford, England. He can be visited at www.dennishamley.com.

INTRODUCING
The Nautilus Series

1. *One Is One* by Barbara Leonie Picard   1-58988-027-7
2. *Pageants of Despair* by Dennis Hamley   1-58988-028-5
3. *The Chess Set in the Mirror* by Massimo Bontempelli
   1-58988-031-5 (forthcoming)

One Is One and *Pageants of Despair* launch **The Nautilus Series** from Paul Dry Books. We think of these titles for young adults like seashells washed up on the beach. As a beautiful shell picked from the sea's edge can fascinate the beachcomber, so the rightly chosen book delights a reader. Such books please the eye, the ear, and the imagination – they seem to arrive from a great distance, bearing wondrous sights and sounds.

We hope that with *One Is One* and *Pageants of Despair* many readers will begin their collections of young adult titles from Paul Dry Books.

BOOKS TO
AWAKEN,
DELIGHT,
&EDUCATE